Blood Feud

Montana gold prospector Luke Driscoll has returned home to Garrison, Texas, when he receives a letter from his estranged brother Nate who has become embroiled in a land dispute with cattle baron Robert McTavish – and it's about to turn deadly. But Luke also meets the lovely Miranda, McTavish's eldest daughter, and cannot help his feelings for her. Now Luke must balance family loyalty and his budding love for Miranda to fight the determined and resourceful rancher, McTavish, and his crew of hired killers.

Blood Feud

Bill Grant

A Black Horse Western

ROBERT HALE

© Bill Grant 2017
First published in Great Britain 2017

ISBN 978-0-7198-2473-9

The Crowood Press
The Stable Block
Crowood Lane
Ramsbury
Marlborough
Wiltshire SN8 2HR

www.bhwesterns.com

Robert Hale is an imprint
of The Crowood Press

Typeset by
Derek Doyle & Associates, Shaw Heath
Printed and bound in Great Britain by
CPI Group (UK) Ltd, Croydon, CR0 4YY

CHAPTER 1

Luke Driscoll hauled on the reins of his gelding. The sprightly horse lurched at the sudden check, then came to a halt. Luke reached into his saddlebag and pulled out his brother's missive. The writing had faded in the three months since he'd received it, and dust and grime coated its surface, but the urgency of the call it carried was undiminished. He shielded his eyes against the fading sunlight and urged his mount forward once more. When Luke got the letter from Nate it had been five years since he last heard from his brother.

Now, at last, he was ready to see him again. Luke had thought there would be a welling-up of emotion in him upon seeing the old family ranch house, but when it came into view he felt nothing. No tears, no lump in the throat, no recalling of fond memories in his mind, nothing.

He had been away too long.

As he made his approach the front door suddenly swung open. A woman stood there. She was wearing a stained dress and her unkempt brown hair was tied back.

5

Her face, though smudged with dark streaks as if she had just come from cleaning the chimney, was attractive. Her gaze pierced through Luke and he would have smiled at her but for the fact that she was cradling a shotgun in her arm. He stopped the horse right in front of the porch and dipped his head in salute.

'Evening ma'am. Is Nate – Nathan – Driscoll at home?'

'Who wants to know?'

Luke chewed the inside of his mouth for a moment before answering.

'His brother. I have a letter. . . .' As he reached for his saddle-bag he heard the shotgun being cocked. 'Nice and slow, ma'am, nice and slow,' he cautioned, 'it's only a letter.'

She said nothing but watched with those icy blue eyes as Luke slowly pulled the letter out, his right hand raised above his head, far away from his gun. He flipped the letter to her, saw it drop by her feet. Without taking her eyes from him or lowering the gun she crouched down and picked it up. She glanced quickly at the contents, then looked at him, her lips turned up in a sneer.

'What took you so long?'

The woman led him through a hallway to the kitchen.

'Have a seat,' she said. 'My name's Maryanne. I'm Nate's wife. We've been married for four years. He'll be along shortly.'

'Where is he?'

'Range riding. Supper's on the stove – it'll be chilli and corn. I can offer you a little whiskey while you wait.'

'Thank you, ma'am.'

She gave him a straight look as she handed him a glass

6

of rye, as though to imply that 'ma'am' was an odd way to address your sister-in-law, but Luke was too tired from the long ride to respond, and anyway, he needed to get used to the idea that Nate had got himself married. He downed the whiskey, then sat silently while Maryanne busied herself around the kitchen.

Soon there came the sound of hoofs crunching on hardpack outside. Maryanne ran out of the kitchen along the hallway to the front door to greet a tall man who was wearing a black fedora. She stretched up to whisper to him quickly, then he followed her as she walked back to the kitchen.

'Nate, this is Luke,' she said. 'He finally came.'

The tall man approached Luke, looking at him as though he were only vaguely familiar.

'Hard to recognize you with that beard,' he said. 'They don't have barbers in Montana?'

Luke scratched the thick growth of hair on his chin. He'd had the beard for so long he didn't even think about it any more. All the men he knew in Montana had beards. There were too few women around to worry about shaving; furthermore, it kept your face warm.

'Or post offices neither?' the tall man pressed his questioning. Luke shrugged. 'It took you long enough to get here.'

Luke regarded his elder brother coldly as Nate sat down opposite him across the table. Maryanne set a plateful of the savoury-smelling chilli and corn before each of them. Luke, famished as he was from his long ride, dug into his food with relish.

'There was a new seam of gold found in a place where it hadn't been expected,' he said. 'Most of the other prospectors had gone on further up north. I had a grub-stake to pay back. I couldn't just up and leave.'

'You can when your family – your only family – calls on you.' Nate's face was twisted in fury. 'It's been five years and not a word from you until now.'

'It cuts both ways, brother. Well, I'm here now. So what is so urgent that you need my help with? Trouble with Comanches?'

'If only.' Nate rubbed his eyes; suddenly he looked tired. 'Why don't you get some rest, Luke? You can take the spare bedroom, and we'll talk in the morning when we're both fresh. One of my hands will take your horse to the stable.'

With that the elder brother stood up and walked away leaving his own food uneaten. Luke only shook his head and downed the last of his whiskey.

The next morning Luke, clean-shaven and with a hair-cut barbered by the merciless hands of his brother's wife, rode silently next to Nate for some distance across the spread.

'We used to have two thousand head of cattle, now I've got a little over a thousand. My land boundaries are up beyond that creek a ways, all the way south of the mesa where we were this morning.' Nate was explaining the situation while they sat, astride their mounts, on top of a ridge.

'How many men you say ride for you?' Luke spoke at last, a bored look in his eye.

'Eight, I told you. I got eight hands. I used to have fifteen but a few got scared away – decided to take their chance on the grub line.'

'We've been riding all day inspecting your lands, but you haven't told me yet what you want from me.'

'That's always been the trouble with you, Luke: no patience. I've lost a lot of cattle and too many good hands because a rival rancher has staked a claim to my lands. He's backed that claim with force – with men who ride for his brand, who steal my cattle and scared away the Bar D's hands. They killed one: ol' Tim Bullard, been with me for years. Made it look like a Comanche raid, but I know it was them. That's why I asked you to come, Luke. I need you to be my *segundo*. Help me win this battle against the McTavishes.'

Luke was silent for a while after Nate finished talking, letting his words sink in. Then he spoke quietly.

'How long has this been going on?'

'Almost two years now since they moved in. I thought I could handle it but I can't. Not without you.'

'The law?'

'What amounts to the law in these parts is smack dab in McTavish's pocket. The Rangers? They might help, but they're too far away and have their own troubles. I need you, Luke, loath though I am to admit that. You're quick with a gun and don't scare easily. Besides, you're family and I can count on you.' Nate gave his brother a pointed look. Luke stared at him.

'I don't know, Nate. It's been a while since I pointed a gun at another man.'

'There's more, though. Maryanne is pregnant. I need protection for her and my baby – just in case. . . .' Nate broke off, the rest of his thoughts remained unspoken.

'All right, Nate, I'll help out,' Luke told him. 'We are family, after all; but darn it, you gotta treat me with respect.'

9

'Don't worry Luke, I'll give you all the respect a ranch *segundo* deserves. Come on, let's get back to the bunkhouse. I'll introduce you to your new hands.'

Luke looked over the eight hands who made up the full complement of employees remaining with his brother. They were a ragtag lot; most were from Texas or New Mexico: drifters trying to earn their bread. Luke didn't know if any of them were gunmen. They looked more desperate than fearless, as though holding on to the Bar D was a last resort.

'So I guess you all are the ranch hands.' Luke said after Nate had left him alone with the group. 'Like Nate said, I'm your new *segundo*. Do you have any questions?'

'How long you been a puncher?' asked one mean-looking ornery cuss, giving him the stink eye.

'To be honest I'm not a cowboy. When my brother sent for me I was up in Montana, where I've been prospecting for the last few years. But that doesn't mean I don't know what's what on a ranch; I'm a quick learner. So I hope you fellows will help me. In the meantime I'm here to watch your backs.'

'So you're a gunhand, eh?' said Ol' Stink-eye, uttering a dismissive grunt.

'No, I'm the *segundo*, and what I say goes around here as far as any of you need concern yourselves. Nate tells me we're having trouble with a neighbor, Robert McTavish, owner of the Rocking M ranch who is rustling large numbers of our beeves. They've got to be stopped, so what I need from each and every one of you is loyalty, You ride for the Bar D brand or you ride on out of here.'

'So that's it, eh?'

'Yeah, that's it, and I'd appreciate it if you wouldn't look at me cross-eyed, Mr. . . ?'

'Taggart, Bob Taggart.'

'Bob, is that square?'

'Yes, sir – Mr Driscoll. I believe it is.'

'Anyone else have any problems with me as *segundo*, or if anyone wants to leave, now's the time. Hit the door and my brother will pay your wages. There's no shame in it; there's likely to be shooting involved; some of you may die.'

No one moved in the small bunkhouse. Taggart spat his tobacco juice into a tin can lying on the floor, but otherwise there was silence.

'Good, that means every one of you rides for the brand. Taggart, you'll continue as foreman.'

Taggart raised his eyebrows at this.

'Now carry on with your ranching chores. After I've talked to my brother about this McTavish fellow we'll decide how we're gonna approach this here problem.'

Luke made for the door, but as he opened it one of the hands shouted out:

'One more question, boss. Can you shoot?'

Without a word Luke whipped around, his .44 in his hand. In the blink of an eye he fired three shots into the makeshift spittoon, causing it to dance in the air. A puncher, Derek Small, stooped and picked up the can, holding it up so that the rest could see. The three bullets had hit the target so close together that it looked as if only one bullet hole decorated the spittoon.

Luke reholstered, tipped his hat and closed the door to the bunkhouse.

CHAPTER 2

'So this old boy McTavish; I guess he's from Scotland or Ireland or somewhere in the Celtic lands. He comes into west Texas saying he's got himself a land grant from the government, says he can set up a ranch anywhere he dad-burned pleases. Only he never lets me see any papers. He plunks himself on land smack-dab next to mine, and says he owns this territory or that territory, even if my cattle been grazing on it for however many years. The sheriff he ain't no help neither, says McTavish has the right of it. So here I am, at deadlock.'

'What do you figure on doing about it?' Luke asked. He and his brother were playing at checkers.

'I hate to think it will come to shooting, but I gotta prepare for that eventuality. No one will intimidate me. This is my land, and I'd rather eat nails than have any Scotsman drive me off it.'

'You think your ranch hands are up for the fight?'

'What do you think? You got a good gander at them.'

'I think they're loyal. I gave them the option to leave, but all of them stayed. Still, it's something else when the lead starts flying. Some of them may scare easily.'

12

'We'll see.' Nate shrugged his shoulders. 'I've never asked much of them. Even during Comanche attacks – though we haven't had many, thank the good Lord. I hired them for their riding and roping skills, not their gun work. Still, I think they can handle themselves in a fight.'

'Good to know, Nate. Since you're giving me liberty to handle this as I see fit, tomorrow I'm gonna scout around McTavish's land, see if I can't poke him a little, see what his intentions are.'

'Now don't go starting no fight, Luke; you always were the hot-headed one.'

'Don't worry, Nate, I'm only going to push him – not too much, but I need to let him know we're not going anywhere. Sometimes you let a bully know you're gonna stand your ground and that's enough to make him back down. I'm hoping that's the case with McTavish.'

'Hoping you're right too, little brother. It's getting late. Think I'll turn in with the missus. 'Night, Luke.'

' 'Night, Nate.'

Luke stayed at the checkerboard, staring at the pieces after his brother had gone to bed, his mind turning over the problem. He wanted to help his brother quickly so that he could go back to Montana. The hot dry air of Texas didn't agree with him. *Yes*, he thought, *tomorrow I'll poke Robert McTavish, see if the bully puts up a fight or not.* It was several years since he'd last been in a fight.

He hadn't told his brother that. Nate remembered him as hot-tempered, which he had been in his youth. Age had mollified him somewhat: that and the love of a good Cheyenne woman, sadly taken by the smallpox three winters ago. He didn't want to return to the

13

impetuousness of his youth, but his brother needed him. The sooner this was over the better.

After a long while sitting in the dark he rose and went to his own bedroom; eventually he drifted off to sleep.

Early the next morning Luke took Taggart and two other men: Doug Eaton and Seamus O'Malley, and rode to the northern boundary of his brother's land.

'Over there is the McTavish spread,' Taggart told him. 'They've been encroaching on us for the past six months. Their cattle mixes in with ours and, any chance they get, they put their brand – the Rocking M – to our herd and then claim them.' Taggart spat as he worked the tobacco in his mouth.

Luke said nothing, only stared at the empty grassland. In the distance he thought he saw a rider.

'How many men does McTavish have?' he asked at last.

'Oh, about twenty-five or thirty I suppose. He runs a big outfit. Thirty against ten, not good odds.'

'Down here is the actual boundary?' Luke pointed to a stand of hickory trees.

'More like here.' Taggart moved his horse back and turned to point to a long line of white rocks. 'Almost every night their outriders come along and scatter or move the rocks and nearly every morning we have to come along and replace them. See here how the line is uneven.'

'Looks like you need a fence.'

'We had a makeshift one; darned thing would blow over in the night. At least that's what McTavish claimed. The boss couldn't afford the manpower to build a fence so we made do with this line of rocks. Not that it does us any good.'

'No good at all. Let me take a look on the other side. Might have a talk with this McTavish fellow.'

Taggart raised his eyebrows but didn't object. Doug and Seamus shifted uneasily in their saddles, darting glances at each other.

Luke sighed. 'You fellows can stay here. If you hear shooting, then run for the ranch and get behind Maryanne's skirts.'

That put steel in their spines. The four men checked their guns for ammo and, following Luke's lead, they stepped over the boundary on to McTavish's land.

As Luke and the ranch hands rode they saw more cattle with the Rocking M brand. They came to a shallow stream where several dozen cows were grazing. Luke pulled up on his reins and turned his head sideways.

'You see any that might be ours that have been rebranded?'

'We'd have to get a closer look; your brother uses the Bar D brand,' Seamus told him.

Before Luke could respond he heard a loud war-whoop, then a shot. He spun his gelding round, his hand already gripping the Colt.

'Comanches?' he yelled at Taggart.

'No, McTavish's men,' came the reply.

The four of them found themselves surrounded by ten men who had come crashing through the trees.

'What do we have here, eh?' cried their apparent leader. 'Looks like trespassers on Mr McTavish's land.'

'Let's string 'em up, Johnny. Make 'em swing; they be rustlers for sure.'

'No, we'll take them back to the ranch; let the boss

15

deal with them.' The man called Johnny sneered at Luke. 'Never seen you before,' he said. 'What in the hell are you doing here?'

'Take me to McTavish and I'll answer his questions . . . not yours.'

Johnny stared at Luke, trying to make the man look away. Eventually, after several tense moments had passed, he relented. He nodded his head.

'Right then, you boys take their guns,' he said; then, to Luke and his companions he added: 'Hand them over nice and easy, don't want you riling up the women folk none.'

Luke nodded to his men and the four of them handed over their Winchesters and Colts. 'Will you gentlemen please follow me,' said Johnny.

McTavish's crew escorted Luke and his men to a low-built but imposing ranch house. It was easily three times as big as Nate and Maryanne's place. Taggart gave out a low whistle and Luke couldn't help but be impressed, nodding in appreciation.

'This here, boys, is La Casa McTavish, home to the richest man in the county. May his justice towards you be merciful,' said Johnny. He stopped his horse, handed the reins to a young ranch hand, ran up the steps and through the ornate doors. Luke and his men sat their horses, half-fearful that they wouldn't be able to make a fast getaway.

Soon Johnny returned, a wide grin on his otherwise rather pinched face. He was followed by a tall, gray-bearded man who was wearing a white Stetson and shiny, brand-new boots. His gaze swept the four men, coming to rest on Luke. His pale blue eyes looked keenly into

Luke's. When he spoke, his accent was a thick Irish brogue.

'My man Johnny says he found you gentlemen sniffing around my cattle, on my land. Will you be having any explanation for your behavior?'

Luke got off his horse, faced the tall man and cleared his throat.

'Forgive us. Mr McTavish, is it?' he said.

The tall man inclined his head slightly.

'Yes. You see, Mr McTavish, you have to understand something. The boundary between your land and my brother's has ... uh ... become confused lately. So we came in to see if some of our cows have likewise become confused as to which herd they belong to.'

McTavish wrinkled his nose and directed a half-sneer at Luke.

'Sir, I assume you must be joking. My brand is clearly marked on all of my cattle, which is prime beef. I breed only the finest steers. I don't have cattle from any other ranch. Which ranch did you say you were from?'

'Driscoll, your next-door neighbor.'

'Driscoll? Oh, yes. He has often complained to me about cattle-mixing. His cattle go missing or Comanches steal them and he blames me. You tell your brother that I have had it with his accusations, so I have. This is your final warning. If he sends any more men or family relations to my land trying to steal my herd, I will have them shot, so I will. Are we clear, Mr Driscoll?'

'Luke – Luke Driscoll is my name.'

'*Luke* Driscoll, did I make myself clear.'

'Clear as crystal, Mr McTavish.'

'Excellent; now leave my sight. Johnny, when they are

17

back on Driscoll territory return their guns to them. You have my orders now on trespassers. Don't bother me again with this imposition.'

'Yes sir.' Johnny turned to the Driscoll men. 'You heard the man; you boys get on out of here. He quick-drew his pistol and pointed it at Luke, an evil grin on his face. Luke, unconcerned, walked back to his horse unhurriedly. As he set himself on the saddle he looked up and noticed a young girl peeking through a window of the ranch house. The sight of her almost took his breath away: fiery red hair, tantalizing eyes, and a face that looked like it belonged on a Renaissance painting.

Luke turned his gaze back quickly to his men, wondering if the mystery girl had seen him. No one had noticed him looking at her, and he tried to put her out of his mind. He didn't try too hard, and thoughts of her preoccupied him on their silent journey back to Nate's ranch house.

Johnny and another of the McTavish ranch hands followed a short distance behind them as far as the line of white rocks. As soon as all four of his men were over the line Luke held up his hand for them to stop. They waited as Johnny approached.

'Next time I see you I'll put lead into you,' Johnny told them as he and his partner handed over the Driscoll men's weapons.

His menacing tone left no doubt that he meant it.

CHAPTER 3

'I can't believe what you did. Of all the stupid stunts you've done . . . you could have gotten shot or strung up by McTavish.'

Luke watched calmly as his brother, waving his arms, paced in front of him.

'What were you thinking?' Nate stopped pacing and stood directly in front of Luke, arms now folded.

'I only wanted to take my measure of McTavish and to find a few of your cows.'

'Yeah? So now what do we do?'

'Nate, do you trust me?'

Nate looked Luke in the eye.

'You're my brother, Luke; of course I trust you.'

'Then let me handle McTavish my way. Give me Taggart, Doug, and Seamus. You keep the rest of the men and go about the ranch business. Don't ask me any questions and I won't involve you or Maryanne. If it gets too hot and the lead starts flying maybe we'll have to pull up stakes.' Luke put up his hand when he saw his brother's frown. 'But it won't come to that. You say you trust me, then trust me, and I'll solve this McTavish problem for you. By the way, does he have any children . . . sons. . . ?'

'No, he doesn't have sons. He has at least one daughter; Miranda is her name. She's in her twenties, I think . . . still young.'

Luke's heart leaped: the girl in the window – she must have been Miranda.

The next day Luke rode into the nearest town, Garrison. It took half a day and by the time he arrived he was starving. He sought out the nearest saloon, tethered his horse to the hitch rail and walked in. The barkeep barely looked at him as he took Luke's order for a whiskey and a steak.

There were about half a dozen patrons, all sitting at tables. Luke sat at the bar and chewed his food thoughtfully; his steak was on the small side and tough but it came with a side of 'taters and greens. The whiskey tasted watery, and the Driscoll ranch's new *segundo* wondered how many people regularly patronized this saloon. He asked the barkeep, who merely pointed to a sign behind the bar: The Lucky Horseshoe, it read. Luke's jaw dropped; maybe the quality of the food and drink served here was just a matter of luck – good or bad.

As he downed a second shot of whiskey the batwing doors swung open. Luke, hearing the clinking of spurs, glanced quickly at the newcomer. The man wore typical trail gear: a duster, a wide-brimmed fedora, unpolished boots, and two tied-down Colts. He moved with confidence, casually and calmly, but his eyes were taking everything in. *A gunslinger*, thought Luke, as the newcomer's roving gaze lit upon him. The stranger walked over and stood by the empty chair right next to Luke.

Luke pointedly ignored him until the man drawled in a heavy Southern accent:

'Is this seat taken?'

Luke shook his head. 'Help yourself, pardner. I was about to head out.'

'Where you headed, cowboy?'

'Not sure if that's a concern of yours.' The hairs on the back of Luke's neck were prickling. This man seemed too inquisitive; he was up to something.

'Hey! Enjoy yourself while you can.'

'Do I know you from somewhere?'

The man looked down at Luke; he noticed that Luke's hand was near his gun.

'Don't reckon I can say as we've met,' he said, 'but no doubt we'll get to know each other real soon.' He seated himself on the chair.

Luke glared at him, then left the saloon.

Whoever he was, the gunslinger had seemed to know something about him. Hired by McTavish? That was a possibility: McTavish would be wary of him now. Perhaps his brother was right: going on to McTavish's land and forcing a direct confrontation had not been the smartest idea. Still, what was done was done; now he'd have to watch his back.

Luke left the saloon and walked his horse to the front of Tanner's general store; There he stopped, patted the shopping list that was tucked into his shirt pocket, then stepped inside.

While Garrison itself was a small town there were homesteads in the surrounding countryside, so the general store kept a steady supply of farming equipment and today it was fully stocked. Luke found most of what he was looking for.

As he fed his horse some oats, preparing him for the ride back home, he saw an ornately painted buckboard pull up to the store. Luke took one look at the driver and forgot all about loading his supplies on to his horse. Out stepped the fiery-haired Miranda McTavish. Her green eyes pierced Luke as she entered Tanner's store. Luke tipped his hat, then on impulse followed her inside.

'Pardon me, ma'am,' he said as he prevented a bolt of material from falling to the floor. Miranda was balancing three more bolts of cloth while the harried store manager trailed her with yet a further two and a sewing kit.

'Miss Miranda,' the man was protesting, 'you're going to buy out all of my cloth.'

'Oh, Mr Tanner! Don't worry; this cloth will keep me well stocked for the next season. I have a lot of sewing to do, Papa needs a new jacket.' She turned and saw Luke clutching the bolt of cloth.

'Oh . . . thank you, kind sir . . . yes, please, just put that on the counter. I'm sorry, I don't actually know your name.'

'Luke, ma'am, Luke Driscoll,' he said. He placed the cloth on the counter, then took Miranda's load from her arms.

'Thank you kindly, Mr Driscoll. I'm Miranda McTavish.'

'I'm pleased to meet you, Miss McTavish'

'I believe I may have seen you before,' the young woman said with a shy smile.

'That may be the case, I had . . . a . . . business meeting with your father yesterday.'

'Yes, now I remember. You're from the Driscoll ranch. The Driscolls are our neighbors.'

'Yes, Miss McTavish. We have a slight dispute over the boundaries of our respective ranges. But I'm sure it's nothing we can't work out. Your father seems a reasonable man.'

'Please – do call me Miranda – but it seems you must not know my father if you think he's reasonable.' Miranda smiled sweetly at Luke. His heart pounded, and sweat formed on his palms.

'Mostly the dispute is between your father and my brother. I only arrived a few days ago from Montana Territory.'

'Only a few days ago?' Miranda's eyebrows rose slightly.

'To help my brother with the ranching. He's lost a few men and can't afford to hire any replacements.'

'I see.' She turned to the storekeeper. 'Thank you, Mr Tanner,' she said as she finished paying. 'Could you wrap everything and place it in my wagon?'

'I'll help you, Tanner,' said Luke. He grabbed two bolts of cloth.

After the two men had finished loading the wagon Luke helped Miranda into the driver's seat.

'Thank you for all your help today, Mr Driscoll,' she said. 'I do hope you won't be a stranger, seeing as how we're neighbors.'

'Why, Miss McTavish – er – Miranda, I would love to come by and see how you've done with your sewing. I would ask you to call me Luke but I don't reckon your father would appreciate that.'

He smiled again.

'Don't worry about Papa, he's all bark and no bite. But if it makes you feel more comfortable perhaps we could have a picnic – away from the ranches?'

Luke couldn't help but grin.

'That sounds mighty fine, Miranda. I might take you up on that offer and come a-calling.'

'I'll look forward to it, Luke.' With that she flicked the reins and her team of horses started off. She waved at the two men. Tanner went back inside his store but Luke stayed watching Miranda's buckboard until at last it disappeared.

When Luke returned home the ranch house was empty. Concerned, he tried the barn, there most of the stalls were empty. As he was returning to the main house he saw Maryanne pulling up in her wagon.

'Hello Luke,' she called, waving to him, 'I just went into town to get a few bags of Arbuckle and other supplies.'

'Hello Maryanne, I didn't know you had gone into town. I just got back from there myself.'

'Oh – did you get something from the store?'

Luke smiled to himself. 'No,' he lied, 'I was on a scouting trip.'

'That's nice, Nathan should be home soon. I think he's checking on the herd. Soon he's going to drive the cattle up to the new stockyards in Abilene.'

Luke nodded, still looking at Maryanne.

'Well,' she said, her eyes turning toward the floor, her cheeks becoming flushed, 'I guess I'll start dinner now.'

'Did Nate ever talk about me?' he asked before she could walk away. 'You know, while I was in Montana?'

'Not much. He mentioned he had a brother and that

24

you two had had a falling-out, but that was it.'

Luke looked at her for a long moment, her eyes met his, unblinking.

'Maybe some day I'll tell you what it was all about,' he said. 'That is, if Nate don't tell you first.'

The sound of approaching hoofbeats made them break off their tête-à-tête.

'Hum, that must be Nate now. I'll – I'll be in the kitchen,' Maryanne said. She had a nervous look in her eye.

Luke went to sit out on the porch, watching as his brother came riding up with all of his hands.

'Dang burn it, Luke! Where in tarnation have you been? We got to get the herd ready to move up to Abilene. We gotta sell the cattle before the market becomes flooded with beefers.'

'I went into town, trying to resolve our little neighbor problem.'

'Yeah? Any luck?'

'Still working on it. When do you plan to leave for Abilene?'

'In a week if there are no hang-ups.'

'All right, I'll be ready.'

'Tell me next time you go into town. I don't want you mucking up this situation worse than it already is.'

'Nate, I'm trying to help you,' Luke said with a sigh.

'I know you are. Anyway, I'm going in to talk to Maryanne. Bright and early tomorrow.'

'Sounds good, big brother. I'll see you at supper time.'

Luke stayed on the porch after Nate had gone inside. He sat down in a rocking chair, pulled out his harmonica and began to play a soft mournful tune.

Miranda hummed to herself all through the dinner preparations. During dinner, while her father droned on about the cattle market and beef prices, she amused herself with thoughts of Luke. He was quite dashing – or so she thought.

'We'll see what happens when we drive the herd to Abilene. Miranda, what is that look on your face? Is something wrong, my dear?'

'Oh, I'm fine, Papa, only lost in thought.'

'Why don't you keep your mind busy and clear the table. Thanks for the dinner, Mama. I'll be outside with my pipe.'

Miranda waited until her father was outside before she stood up and started taking the dishes to the kitchen.

'Lost in thought?' her mother echoed. 'More like lost in love.'

Miranda looked askance at her mother, opened her mouth to protest, but her mother cut her off with a shake of her head.

'No, darling, I know that look. I've been there with your father. Cupid's arrow has smitten you.'

'It has, Mama.' Miranda smiled sheepishly. 'I met a man today when I went to the general store.'

Her mother nodded knowingly.

'What's his name?'

'His name . . . his name shall remain a mystery for now until I get to know him better, and I've figured out how to tell Papa.'

'Your father loves you very much, Miranda, and he knows that sooner or later you'll marry. I think he was hoping for later.'

Miranda winced, but her mother didn't seem to notice.

'I'll tell Papa soon, if . . . if he comes a-courting.'

'We will look forward to meeting him.'

Miranda made no further reply and her mother went into the kitchen.

Miranda hoped she wasn't making a mistake. Luke seemed like a kind man, but the dispute between his brother and her father hung like a cloud over her thoughts. She knew in her head what she should do, but her heart was telling her something different.

In such a conflict Miranda knew she would follow her heart.

CHAPTER 4

A week went by without further incident from McTavish or his men. The Driscolls and their hands started slowly gathering up the herd ready to drive it north. One morning Luke and his brother were riding the range together near the edge of Nate's land. 'I don't want any more trouble, Luke. Keep clear of McTavish's spread. I only want to get these beefers up to the railhead, then maybe I'll cash out.'

'You can't quit, Nate. You can't let McTavish win.'

'This ain't a game. I've got a wife – and a baby on the way. I can't let Maryanne become a widder. Your job now is to make sure I don't lose any more cattle.'

'Sure thing, big brother. I'll help you out. Why, lookee here . . .' Luke looked off into the distance, Nate's gaze following his. Four men were riding toward them, herding half a dozen cows.

'Hello,' Luke called, 'have you found our missing cattle?'

'I don't think they're our men, Luke,' Nate cautioned. As the men rode closer he could make out for sure that they weren't hands of the Driscoll ranch.

'Stay where you are,' he called.

Luke took out his shotgun from its scabbard and readied his pistol. Nate, eyeing the men nervously, did the same. The four men continued riding as if they hadn't heard Nate, so he hollered yet again. This time one of the men looked up. Pointing to Nate and Luke, he shouted to his companions.

Together the four punchers rode away from the beefers and charged the Driscoll brothers. Nate tried to work his gun out of its holster but Luke was faster. Two shots cracked from the shotgun and he felled two of the punchers. The other two wheeled away, heading for McTavish's spread. Luke and Nate rode up to the two unhorsed men. Both had been able to get to their feet, though they were obviously in pain.

'Hey, I only nicked you. Consider it a warning. What about those cattle, Nate?'

Nate was looking over the cows, which had moved some distance away to continue their grazing.

'Yup, they're mine. I recognize my brand.'

'Hell no! Those are McTavish's. You stole 'em, Driscoll. We was just coming to get back our rightful property,' one of the men said. He stood up, holding his arm.

'Any proof of that accusation?' Nate asked.

'We don't need to give you proof; the sheriff will hear about it.'

'Chief, you tell McTavish that if he can provide proof these cows were stolen from him, and not the other way around, then maybe I'll give you an apology for shooting you. Now get out of here, 'afore I change my mind and decide it'd be better to put you both six feet under.'

After some moments hesitation the two McTavish men remounted their horses and rode off after their *compadres*. When they were out of sight, Nate turned to his brother.

'Thanks Luke,' he said. 'If it weren't for your quick shooting, I might have been dead.'

'Yeah, those boys were looking for blood. It was bold of them to come out in the day like that, herding our beeves if they were their own.'

'McTavish must think no one will oppose him. Another reason I was thinking of pulling up stakes. There's too much risk for me with Maryanne.'

'Don't worry, Nate, I'll deal with this trouble. I don't want you getting cold feet now, you hear? I'll need you to stand firm with me against him. If you run that'll be the end of it, your herd, your land, your men – they'll all be gone. Now, it might be best to send Maryanne away somewhere. But you – you've got to stay.'

'That's fine, Luke, I'll stay. But I'll talk to Maryanne about her leaving in case it gets too rough. Her sister lives in Austin. She should be safe there.'

'Good, Nate. Now let's round up our herd.'

They gathered together the six beefers and gently nudged them toward the main herd. Luke couldn't help thinking, though, that sooner or later this land feud with McTavish would come to a head, with blood being spilled.

Miranda peered out of the window as her father's men came galloping back. She could see only two: Jake and Birch, she thought they were. They rode up almost to the porch and pounded on the door.

'Mr McTavish, come quick,' they hollered.

'What's the matter, Jake?' Miranda heard her father say.

'Ambushed – the damned Driscolls – we were gathering up our strays on their land and they damned near killed us.'

'Where are the others?'

'We saw Eric and Zeb get hit – don't know what happened to them.'

'The cows?'

Jake shook his head, 'Driscoll's got 'em.'

'Round up the boys,' said McTavish. 'It's time to put an end to this land dispute.'

Soon the injured drovers came riding back, both of them bleeding and clearly riding in some discomfort. They dismounted and stumbled into the ranch house, where Miranda had to act as nurse after fetching water for the blacksmith, who now acted as a surgeon. She didn't know if Luke had been involved in the shooting, but she feared for his safety. Despite what she had told Luke, she knew that her father could sometimes be a ruthless man. Miranda only hoped that this dispute would end quickly, without any more unnecessary bloodshed.

Her father's foreman, Zachary Thompson, often shared her father's outlook; he could be a hard man and was completely loyal to McTavish. They had known each other during the war. Now he stood next to her father on the porch with more than twenty ranch hands gathered before them. Miranda stood back in the doorway, near her mother and sisters, to listen as Zack spoke.

'Now men, we've got ourselves a problem. Those

damned upstarts on the Driscoll spread have done gone and shot up our men. This is an unprovoked attack that must be answered. I'm looking for volunteers to ride for the brand and teach Driscoll once and for all that he can't steal our cattle and he can't shoot our men. Who's with me?'

All the men shouted; three or four drew their pistols and fired in the air. Zack nodded to McTavish, then mounted a horse. Twenty riders followed his example and galloped away uttering whoops and hollers. Only when they were beyond his sight did McTavish come back into the house. He sat down heavily in his chair, his wife put a drink in his hand. After a long pull, he sighed.

'I'm sorry, Miranda,' he said, 'that you had to see all that, you and your sisters. I was hoping it wouldn't come to this, but Nate and his brother, they didn't give me any other choice.'

'But Papa, isn't that land theirs? Aren't we stealing their cows?'

'The land deeds are not clear, darling. When I made my claim I thought it was a modest stake. But Driscoll says he was here first, and he claimed the whole damn valley. It wasn't fair.'

'But Papa,' Miranda ventured, risking her father's anger, 'isn't Texas big enough for both of us? Why, there's plenty of land. We can share, can't we?'

'There is a lot of land, true, Miranda, but not all of it is good for grazing cattle. There's water near by, and in case of drought that's vital. No, Miranda, this land is prime, my herd is bigger so Driscoll has to make way. He wouldn't, so now I'm going to force him. Zack's a good man, he knows what he's doing. Hopefully, no one else will get hurt and all this will be over soon.'

'And what if it isn't?'

Her father turned his eyes away. He looked into the distance for a long moment, then fe said softly:

'There's another way.'

He finished his drink and followed Miranda's doting mother into the bedroom.

'They're going to come, I tell you,' said Luke as he cleaned his rifle.

Nate nodded, 'I know. Are the men ready?'

'They're ready. You should get Maryanne to safety.'

'She says she won't leave for Austin but she'll stay in the cellar.'

'That's good enough. Now help me board up the windows.'

The two brothers and their hands worked diligently to secure the ranch house. Horses were corralled, windows boarded up and doors barricaded. Luke was certain that McTavish wouldn't let this latest incident pass unchallenged. He had looked into the man's eyes and seen hard steel and iron there. There was no relenting in the man. He only hoped Nate knew that. He had tried to impress the urgency of the situation upon his brother, but Nate couldn't see the situation the way Luke did. He believed that McTavish could still be reasoned with, might even be prepared to give way after this latest incident. So Maryanne could stay; Nate probably hadn't even asked her to go, and was risking her and her unborn child's lives.

There is nothing for it now but to wait, thought Luke.

They waited.

Three of the ranch hands, Doug and Seamus and Slim Jim Tucker were holed up in the main house with Luke and Nate. Maryanne was hiding in a disused cellar adjacent to the house. Luke had ordered the other five hands to hide in a small copse of hickories a few hundred feet away. No sense in getting everyone trapped in the same place. When McTavish's men came, they'd be ready for them. Soon Luke heard the telltale drumming of hoofs that signaled their arrival.

'Driscoll, I know you're in there. This is Zachary Thompson, Robert McTavish's foreman. I've come to hold you personally responsible for the injuries caused to two of Mr McTavish's men. Surrender yourself and your brother and we will take you to the sheriff.'

'Go to hell, Thompson.'

'So be it. Boys!'

Gunfire erupted. Luke, Nate and their men stayed flat on the floor as bullets whizzed through the makeshift barricades. Once the volley had stopped the Driscoll men jumped up, picked up their rifles and, using gun slits, answered back. Luke saw McTavish's men scatter, and as he had predicted one of them began lighting a torch.

'We'll smoke 'em out,' said Thompson.

Luke let out a war cry between shots, answered by the men behind the copse with a hail of gunfire. Now McTavish's men found themselves caught in the middle of the crossfire. They panicked and fled as their horses tried desperately to escape the terrible sounds of the guns. Luke jumped out on to the porch, firing his Henry repeating rifle at the fleeing men. He saw one man look back, trying to rally the others; figuring it was Thompson he shot the man's hat off his head. That did it; there was no more fight left in them. The rest hightailed it back to McTavish's land.

'Good job, Luke. You did it.' Nate clapped Luke on the back.

'I don't know how events got out of hand, Nate, but I fear we've made matters a whole lot worse.'

Five men lay dead. All of them McTavish's.

'Now what?' asked Seamus as he came through the front door. Luke and Nate surveyed the scene.

'Damnation!' Nate swore. 'We'd better get the sheriff.'

'No, Nate,' Luke said. 'I'm sure we need the Rangers now.'

'I reckon you're right. This is one hell of a mess.'

'They'll be coming hard now. You better make your case before the law. Before you end up in a coffin.'

Nate nodded. 'This is my land and I won't be driven off it, but Maryanne needs to be safe. I don't want her to lose the baby. I'll come back with the law. It'll take me two days to get to Austin. In five days I'll return.'

'What should I do with the bodies?'

'Round up their horses and send them back to McTavish so he can bury them.'

'That sounds like a good idea.'

'When are you leaving?'

'As soon as possible.'

Luke watched his brother go to find Maryanne, then he ordered the men to load the dead men on to their horses as Nate had suggested.

'If their mounts have already gone home put the bodies in a wagon and take them to the boundary line. McTavish's boys can find them from there.'

Luke didn't know what he had gotten himself into. He

knew there was only one way this would end, in blood-shed.

He just hoped the blood wasn't his own.

CHAPTER 5

Her father was in a foul mood. Miranda could see him practically steaming after Zack and the remainder of the men returned. She didn't need to hear the conversation to know that their mission had turned out badly for them. Still, she edged closer to the half-closed door of her father's study, where the two men were sitting.

'I can get some more men together and burn down their ranch house. Smoke 'em out,' she heard Thompson say.

'No need, Zack. I'll take it from here. I have an ace up my sleeve that will finish off our Driscoll problem once and for all.'

'Boss! Hey boss! Sorry, Miss Miranda, I didn't see you there.' One of the hands had lurched into the doorway, almost hitting Miranda as she scrambled out of the way.

'What is it, Felton? Miranda what are you doing – oh, never mind. Go and check on your mother.'

'Boss, we found a wagon, unhitched, near one of our cow herds. . . .' Felton stopped to catch his breath.

'And?' McTavish said impatiently.

'It's full of bodies, five of 'em.'

'That would be our boys. At least they've done us the

courtesy of sending them back to us,' said Zack, a resigned note in his voice.

'Take them to the undertaker in Garrison and notify their families, Zack. I'll be back.' McTavish's face looked grim.

'Where are you going, Papa,' asked Miranda as her father stomped out of the house.

'To play some cards.'

Luke rode into town again. He saw Nate and Maryanne off as they headed north to Austin. Seamus went with them, in case McTavish had ideas about ambushing Nate on the trail. Nate had persuaded Luke to try the sheriff one more time, to see if he would do anything about McTavish. Luke had told him it would be futile; still, it gave him a good excuse to go into town on the off-chance that Miranda might be there.

He hitched his horse outside the same saloon in Garrison. As he pushed through the batwings a shadow appeared beside his own. He spun around, gun drawn.

'Easy partner, I'm only looking for a drink. Same as you.' Luke found he was facing the gunslinger with the Southern drawl whom he'd met the other day. Now his hands were raised, though his smile suggested amusement rather than alarm.

'Sorry mister,' said Luke. 'You startled me.'

'You seem on edge. Let me buy you a drink.'

The two of them sat down, Luke making certain that his back was to the wall.

'What's your name, stranger?' Luke asked as the barmaid brought them each a glass of whiskey.

'My name is Beaufort – Reginald Beaufort, I'm from

New Orleans. And you?'

'Luke, Luke Driscoll, late of Montana, here now to help my brother.'

'Your brother?'

'Rancher, having a problem with another rancher.'

'Indeed? A range war, then. Sounds exhilarating.'

'So what else are you doing here in Garrison – besides drinking at the saloon.'

'Looking for excitement.' There was a dangerous twinkle in Beaufort's eye that almost made Luke reach for his gun again.

'There's nothing exciting happening here.'

'Except for your range war?'

'No, even that is not exciting, or even interesting. Look, Mr Beaufort. . . .'

'Reginald, please call me Reginald.'

'All right, Reginald, I want to thank you for the drink, but I should be going now,' Luke said. He stood up.

'Back to the range war, eh?'

'No, the general store. I have to get supplies.' Luke gave him an irritated look.

The gunslinger leaned back, one arm dangling over the top rail of the chair, his gun within easy reach. He smiled again. Luke found Beaufort's gaze unnerving; his hand was itching to reach for his iron.

After a long pause Beaufort spoke again, his voice low.

'Yes, you're right, this town is boring. Pray tell me where can I find something more dangerous to do.'

'You don't want to look for trouble, Mr Beaufort, because it might find you,' said Luke. Giving the man a hard look he backed slowly out of the Lazy Horseshoe, never taking his eye away from the gunman.

'I might take a look anyway,' said Beaufort. ' 'Bye, Mr Driscoll.'

Luke was out of the saloon before those last three words had been uttered. He unhitched his horse and galloped away. Not until he was well out of town did he realize that he was sweating. Something about that man had unnerved him. A professional gunman, maybe, who had marked Luke as a target?

Miranda went out riding alone that day. She had to get away from the house; her father was obsessed about the Driscolls. She still had not told him she had met Luke, afraid of what his reaction might be. She hoped she might run into Luke so, intentionally, she rode toward the Driscoll spread. By noon, however, she was lost. Miranda had slowed her horse, casting her gaze about for some recognizable landmark, when she heard a rustling sound in the brush. A bouquet of startled pheasants were taking flight. Miranda turned to watch the elegant birds soaring into the air.

Suddenly a thwack sounded and she felt a sharp pain in her leg. Her claybank reared and bucked, throwing Miranda to a hard landing on the ground.

A war cry whooped, and she knew she was under attack.

Comanches! A band of warriors in full war paint were approaching. She tried to scream, but her throat was too dry.

Then she heard the sharp report of a rifle. One of the warriors, unhorsed, tumbled to the ground. He seemed to her to be lifeless: his tongue was lolling out of his mouth.

She closed her eyes to the horror.

Another rifle sounded and the remaining braves scattered. Soon she heard voices speaking English; she wondered whether her father's men had found her. The pain in her leg was becoming intense, she didn't want to open her eyes, couldn't bear to see any more bodies. She felt hot breath on her neck, then she could feel nothing at all.

When she awoke, she was lying on a couch; her wound was dressed and a damp cloth lay on her forehead. She tried to stand up, only to find that her wounded leg couldn't support her and that she was feeling woozy. Frustrated, Miranda collapsed back on to the couch. Moments later she heard footsteps and the faint jingle of spurs.

'Ah, Miss Miranda. You're awake.' A smiling face was looking down on her. Her heart skipped a beat. It was Luke!

'Why, Mr Driscoll! Where am I? What happened?'

'You are in my brother's ranch house. As for what happened, you rode rather close to a Comanche hunting party. Luckily, a few of my hands and I were riding the range and we heard their war cries.'

'Were you looking for Comanches?'

Luke rubbed his head and avoided her eyes.

'No; we were looking for your father's men. We were armed and ready – one of my men is a crack shot. We had scared them off, so it was good fortune that we found you.'

'I am eternally grateful for your assistance, Mr Driscoll.'

'Call me Luke, and – ah – it was no problem.'

'My leg. . . ?'

'Don't worry, it is only a flesh wound. A Comanche tomahawk nicked you. It didn't hit the bone, but it might be best not to walk for a few days, to let it heal.'

'Why, Luke, are you a doctor? Or do you only desire the pleasure of my company?'

'No, ma'am, I'm no doctor, but I've seen enough wounds in my life, on both horses and men, to know what's serious and what's not. And, much as I would enjoy the pleasure of your company, I fear your father will worry about you. What is more, he might blame me – or more likely my brother – for causing the attack and accuse us of kidnapping you. No, it's best to get you back home as soon as you are able to move. In the meantime you are my guest; if there's anything you need, please let me know.'

'Where are your brother and his wife?'

'They are not here at the moment. Still, I'm a decent chef, though nowhere near as good as Maryanne. You'll have to put up with my cooking for the duration of your stay with us.' He held up one finger, as though bidding her to be patient, and left the room. He returned in a few moments, bearing a tray with a teapot, cup and saucer, and biscuits on a plate.

'If you need anything else, give a holler,' he said.

'This should be more than sufficient, mist . . . Luke.' She smiled at him. He smiled back but the colour in his face seemed to be rising. He nodded his head to her, then left her once again.

She realized that she was sitting in a room at the front of the house, near the door. The house seemed rather quaint, modest in size compared to her family's.

Luke had left the house through the front door, so now she was alone. She sipped the tea, which was cooling rapidly, and munched on the dry biscuits. She wondered what her father would say if he could see her now.

She gave a little smile.

'What we will do about her?'

'We can't let her go anywhere until she's fully healed.' Luke answered the speaker, Burt Wiley, one of his brother's less savory ranch hands.

'What about her father? He catches wind of this there will be hell to pay.'

'You let me handle McTavish and his daughter. I need you boys to get ready to drive the herd. With Nate gone I'm going to have to stay here. So it will up to the rest of you to move the herd to market.'

'There's too few of us to drive this herd to Abilene.'

'For now, let me figure out how to do that, Burt.'

'It sounds like you've got a lot of figuring to do. You've got to handle McTavish, his daughter, the ranch, the herd, the Comanches. Maybe you don't need us any more, maybe you can do it on your own.'

'You want to tell me something, Burt?' Luke gave him his hardest, coldest stare.

Burt stepped back from Luke's fierce gaze but still tried to hold his ground.

'I didn't sign up to be shot at on a daily basis. I under-stand loyalty to the brand but money talks. Loyalty ain't gonna help me if I'm six feet under. I can't spend nothing if I'm dead.'

Luke continued to eye the cowboy. The man was

heavyset but moved with a fluency that belied his bulk. Luke figured he could get Burt to the ground if they scrapped, but he didn't want to do that; he knew Burt was right. Reluctantly he looked away. Burt signaled his small victory with a wide grin.

'OK, Burt, but let me tell you something, and this goes for everyone else here.'

Luke turned around to look at his brother's seven ranch hands. 'I understand the risks involved in this land feud. Some of you have only been with the Driscolls for a short time. No one is holding you here. If you want to go, then go. No one's going to judge you. But if you stay, if you help fight for the brand, for my brother and his family, then there's a stake in it for you.'

Luke swallowed hard, his mouth had moved before he'd thought through what he was saying. Too late now, he pressed on.

'That's right, a stake. A land stake. If we beat the McTavish outfit and get our cows to market I'll make sure you all get a piece of the action. Get to buy a plot of land and have cows of your own.'

'Did Nate say you could do that?'

'He knows what I'm doing. I can act by any means necessary to keep this ranch alive. So, as I said before, it's your choice: leave and be gone for good or stay and help finish what we've started.'

There was a murmuring among the men, then Burt stepped forward.

'I think I speak for all of us when I say we'll stay and ride for the brand . . . for a stake in the ranch.'

'Excellent. Now, boys, let's get to work. I need some of you to get the herd ready and some of you to keep your eyes open for McTavish's men. I'll . . . uh . . . I'll see to Miss Miranda.'

Luke waited to see the men start working, then he trudged slowly back to the house, hoping that his brother would understand what he had done.

CHAPTER 6

Robert McTavish was in a frenzy. His eldest daughter was missing. Miranda had last been seen riding away on her claybank.

'You have to find her, Zack,' he roared.

'The last we saw her she said she was going for a ride, then she headed toward the Driscoll spread.'

'That's the wrong answer, Zack. Her poor mother is so distraught. Find her now.'

'I'll get the boys out, the dogs too.'

After his foreman had left Robert poured himself a stiff Scotch and sank into his rocking chair. He knew Zack would do his best but right now his foreman's best wasn't good enough. He had already failed the rancher once, McTavish couldn't afford another failure. He went into the bedroom, where he found his wife lying on the bed, softly weeping. His two other daughters were standing quietly next to her. He opened his mouth as if to speak, but he couldn't find the words. Quietly he left.

He saddled his horse and rode hard into Garrison. He hadn't wanted to call upon the man he was about to see.

Not yet, anyway. He had been hoping to save him for later. But with Miranda missing – and possibly in the hands of Driscoll – he knew he had no choice.

It was nightfall by the time he reached the town. The gunslinger he wanted to find was known to haunt saloons, so he tried the saloon first. He walked through the batwing doors and glanced around. Out of the corner of his eye he saw a tall, finely dressed gentleman lounging languidly at a table near the back of the saloon. His style of dress belied the dangerous look in his eyes. Wasting no time McTavish stepped straight up to the table and pulled out a chair. Sitting across from him McTavish tried to match the other man's steady gaze; he found he couldn't.

'You Beaufort?' he managed to utter.

'I am, and who wants to know?'

'I'm McTavish.'

'Ah, my would-be employer. Where have you been? The last I heard from you I was to wait here in Garrison for further instructions.'

'Now is the time for further instructions. I have a problem.'

'Obviously. That would be the reason you sent for me.'

'The problem's just got bigger. My daughter is missing, possibly kidnapped by the miscreant I want you to deal with it.'

'So?'

'So, deal with him and return my daughter alive and unharmed.'

'Unsullied, you mean.'

'Preferably, but alive will do.' McTavish looked around, 'Do it now.'

'The fair lady's name?'

'Miranda. Check the Driscoll ranch.' McTavish threw a small bag filled with fifty-dollar coins on the table. 'Half-payment now. The rest will be paid on the safe delivery of my daughter.'

'Indeed, I shall do my best. I appreciate your patronage of Reginald Beaufort, gunslinger for hire.'

McTavish grimaced. 'Keep your voice down. I have to get back to my own ranch. Bring her back there as soon as you can. Miranda can guide you.'

The gunman nodded and McTavish left. He hoped he wasn't making a mistake, but he was desperate. He stopped briefly to talk to the sheriff, discreetly greasing the man's palm. On the ride home he started to relax. If this Beaufort was as good as advertised, perhaps he could kill two birds with one stone. See Miranda safely returned and get rid of the Driscolls once and for all.

Robert McTavish permitted himself a small smile as he rode up to his imposing ranch house.

By the second day of her convalescence Miranda was thoroughly enjoying herself. Luke proved to be as charming as he was handsome, providing her with excellent companionship. She wasn't looking forward to her eventual departure from the Driscoll ranch. She was contentedly sipping tea when Luke bustled into the house.

'How ready do you think you are to ride?' he asked, with no niceties as to how she was feeling.

'Why, I'm not sure; my leg does feel better but I haven't spent a great deal of time walking on it. Why do you ask?'

'Because we might have to move you in a hurry. My outriders have reported that your father is sending men this way. A lot of men. I guess you're missed at the McTavish *hacienda.*'

'Oh dear! What are we going to do?'

'*We* aren't going to do anything. You are going back to your father, and I have to figure out a way to get his men not to shoot at us.'

'I suppose that's agreeable, Luke. So when do you plan to deliver me to my father?'

'Right now it's a little awkward. I'll have to figure out how we can do this without inflaming the situation further.'

Luke looked like he was about to say something more, but the pounding hoofs of a galloping horse interrupted him. Miranda tensed as Luke hurried outside. Peeking through the window she could see his agitation clearly as he talked to the mounted man. When he came back inside she knew what he would say to her.

Miranda pouted slightly; Luke's tone was playful.

'Change of plans: we have to leave now. Apparently your father didn't take long to figure out where you'd gone. He's sending out what looks like his whole crew here. We can't stay. Are you able to walk?'

Miranda stood up unsteadily; her leg was still aching.

'I'll manage,' she said through gritted teeth.

'Let's get you on a horse. I don't suppose your father will listen to reason and accept that this is a misunderstanding – that we're not kidnapping you?'

'I don't know, Luke. Daddy's gone real crazy about you and your brother recently. I'm afraid I can't predict what he will do – honestly.'

'That's understandable. If you don't mind you can come with us until we can sort things out with your father. If you'll oblige us, ma'am.' Luke doffed his hat in an almost comical way. Miranda couldn't hide her smile at his awkward charm.

'Why, I'd be delighted to accompany you, Luke.'

He smiled. 'While you prepare yourself I've got to oversee my hands. We'll be pulling up stakes as fast as possible.'

He touched his hat once more, then hurried out through the door.

Miranda was left wondering what she had gotten herself mixed up in. Now she was aware that she was choosing a side in this boundary dispute: it was not the one she had expected.

Luke had left Miranda in a hurry. His scout, Martin, had told him that the whole McTavish outfit was coming fast and hard. He had seen at least thirty riders. Luke couldn't ask his men to stand against that onslaught, and trying to reason with McTavish now would be pointless. The man was clearly gunning for Luke and Nate. So he decided to do the only thing he could do: run. He barked orders at the hands, telling them to get a wagon ready, prepare extra horses, gather some essential tools, and protecting the herd. He didn't expect to return to the ranch house, and Nate would be lucky if McTavish didn't burn it to the ground.

The hands worked diligently, gathering as many supplies as they could, hitching a team to a wagon. Luke sent two outriders to harry McTavish's crew, thus buying them some valuable time. When all was ready he pulled the wagon up to the house.

'In case riding a horse would be too much strain on your leg you can ride in this here wagon,' he told her.

'Thank you, Luke,' said Miranda as he helped her into the back.

'Mount up, boys. Go! Go! Go! Hurry, that crew will be right behind us.' Luke leapt into his saddle and waited until the last of his riders had roared past him.

He had one more trick up his sleeve. He had brought with him sticks of dynamite from Montana. Now he pulled one out of his saddlebag, lit the fuse with a match and hurled it as far away as he could toward McTavish's men. The resulting explosion was deafening, only his steady hand kept his horse from bolting. The pursuing cowboys were thrown into confusion by the blast. 'Let's move out,' he said to Miranda.

Luke now led a ragtag band complete with hostage. A willing hostage, but a hostage, nonetheless. He wondered if they would now be branded as outlaws, hunted by the law as well as by McTavish. He had let the feud get out of hand as his brother's *segundo*, despite his brash words earlier.

Damn! he thought, *at least it can't get any worse.*

Early morning saw the group far to the south of the Driscoll ranch. They had traveled through the night, having no care which way they went as long as they were a safe distance away from McTavish's riders.

Luke looked around. They had stopped on top of a small mesa. From here they could see signs of pursuit in plenty of time to keep ahead of McTavish's men. He reckoned they had come fifty miles and were now deep into

Comanche territory. He hoped they had enough guns to defend themselves if they should run into a war party. Luke had no idea where the nearest ranch was, or even if there were any at all near by. He only wanted to get away from McTavish. Eventually, he figured to double back and head to Garrison or the nearest Ranger station. For now, they would head south.

'Let the horses rest another few hours. I don't think they would have had enough supplies to keep following us. They'd have to go back and gear up before they came into Comanche territory. Miss Miranda, how are you feeling?'

'I'm fine, Luke. My leg is feeling better. Where are we?'

'Far from your father's men, going into Comanche territory. Don't worry, we'll double back and head toward the town where you can see a proper doctor.'

'When will that be?'

'Soon, once I know we're safe.'

'From my father or from the Comanches?'

'Both. A couple of the hands are cooking breakfast. If you would like any coffee please help yourself. I'll be right back.'

Talking to Miranda always made him nervous. He tripped over his tongue and, despite her politeness, he didn't know what she thought of her circumstances. She hadn't been riding to see him, only riding away when the Comanche attacked her. If he hadn't been close by she would have been killed, or worse. Now she was his captive as he fled from the fury of her father. Not exactly the way to win over a lady, he thought ruefully.

Then, banishing these gloomy thoughts, he focused on finding the best route out of this hostile territory before events got worse.

CHAPTER 7

All that day Luke scouted the surrounding land while Miranda and his men slept. He could see no sign of McTavish's men, or of any Comanches. The Indians were only defending their land, something Luke's brother would certainly understand. Still, they were ferocious in that defense of their ancestral homes, so Luke hoped his group wouldn't run into a war party. *One more day maybe,* he thought, *and then I'll double back.* As the sun started to set he came back to the makeshift camp. Everyone was awake and standing around.

'Let's ride,' he told them.

'We're not staying here?'

'Nope, we ride at night. Keep them off our trail.'

'But the horses. . . ?'

Luke held up his hand, 'Don't worry, our path will be straight, they won't go lame.'

At least he hoped they wouldn't. Traveling at night had advantages, and Luke needed all the advantages he could get. There was still grumbling from the men but they packed up the camp and readied their horses without too much serious complaining.

They kept heading south. Luke was unsure of when to turn back; he figured his gut would tell him. After a few hours, drifting between sleep and wakefulness as he meandered on, he was suddenly jerked awake by his horse's whicker.

'Keep your eyes sharp, boys,' he alerted his men. 'We might have company.'

Luke readied his pistol in anticipation. The ranch hands looked around, their eyes darting. Suddenly he heard a war whoop, then an arrow streaked through the air, landing beyond the group. A rifle thundered and Luke had to steady his mount, then he barked out orders.

'Don't let them surround us. *Fire!*'

The scene was chaotic as the Comanches came at them from all sides. Without realizing it they had ridden into a shallow gully, the perfect spot for an ambush. Luke kept firing his pistol as he wheeled his horse, trying to keep the wagon in view. His one concern was keeping Miranda safe. Martin, who was now driving the wagon, was whipping the horses, trying to get free of the ambush. The horses were close to panic, but they complied with the bullwhip and charged forward, running over two braves who were on foot. Seeing that the wagon was now free Luke swung his concentration to the war band. In quick succession he drilled two braves before he reloaded. He wanted his men to rally around the wagon and keep moving south, but no one was listening to him.

Slowly, yet inexorably, the Driscoll ranch hands turned the tide. The Comanches were used to launching hit-and-run raids on isolated farm houses and ranches that they could get to and leave quickly. Having come up against well-armed and desperate men they had now had their fill and they began to withdraw. The last braves sent out parting shots, arrows and gunfire, before the field cleared.

Luke drew in a deep breath.

'Let's check the wagon,' he said.

'We lost a few, boss,' said Doug quietly.

'How many and who?'

'Burt was gunned, and so was Derek. Jim Tucker got shot up bad, don't think he's gonna make it.'

Tarnation! he thought, Derek was a good man and Burt, well, even ol' Burt had come around finally. He couldn't afford to lose many more men.

'Is that all? All right then, Doug; we'll have to bury them here. We can't take them back, and I won't leave them as food for the coyotes. How's the wagon?'

'It's over that hill. Our supplies and Miss Miranda are safe.'

Luke let out a breath. 'We've got to clear out of here before the Indians regroup and come back. Transfer Jim to the wagon. Let's hope he can hold on until we get help.'

'What'll we do now, boss?' asked Doug.

'My gut's telling me that now's a good time to turn around and head for Garrison.' *Before I lose anyone else,* he left the thought unspoken.

Luke wanted to get Miranda back to Garrison as quickly as possible. His hands did not object to leaving Comanche territory as they turned the wagon eastward for several miles, then north again. Their tracks would be easy enough to find if McTavish were still trailing them, but he hoped they had given up the chase by now. To make sure he zigged and zagged his group to confuse their trail.

The Comanches did not reappear and two days without incident brought them to the outskirts of Garrison.

'Looks like we made it. Miranda, do you think you're able to ride? I'm not sure if we should ride into Garrison, your father may have men waiting there.'

Luke smiled at Miranda as she acknowledged she was feeling much better. He was about to offer her his hand as she stepped off the wagon when he heard a shot. Instinctively he ducked his head as his hat was blown off with a dime-sized hole in it. Spinning around, he reached for his gun. Another shot landed near his feet, causing him to jump.

'Now now, Mr Driscoll, I gave you fair warning that I would look for danger. Looks like I found it.'

Luke looked up and saw the gunslinger Beaufort, sitting on a black roan, his hand holding a pearl-handled revolver in his hand. Doug, Martin and the other hands reached for their guns.

'Let's not any of us be too hasty lest I put several bullet holes into your boss's chest.' Beaufort gave a wicked grin. The men looked uncertainly at Luke who grabbed Miranda's hand and pulled her away from the wagon.

'Get down now,' he hissed.

The movement distracted the mounted man; he paused, indecision written on his face. The Driscoll ranch hands opened fire, but the gunslinger had already dived for cover using his horse as a shield. His indecision gone. Beaufort had found a cluster of boulders to hide behind while his horse scampered away.

Shots rained all around, but Luke managed to pull Miranda on to a horse.

'Ride!' He slapped the hindquarters of the beast and watched it charge off at a gallop straight toward Garrison. He breathed more easily now that she was out of harm's way. It had all happened so fast he hadn't had time to think about what he was doing. *Too late now, she's safe*, he kept telling himself, hoping he'd believe it.

He realized now that the gunfire had stopped.

'What's wrong?'

'He's running away,' replied Doug.

'Toward the town?' Luke's heart sank as he thought of Miranda falling into the clutches of the gunslinger.

'No, the other way – east. Maybe we scared him off.'

'Yeah, maybe,' said Luke, not believing a word of it.

Doug was right, though; the man who called himself Beaufort had recaptured his horse and was riding hard north, away from the town.

Miranda felt exhausted as she rode into Garrison. Her horse, lathered in sweat, could barely keep going. The town seemed to be further away than she had thought when she left Luke fighting the gunman; time dragged as she rode.

At last she was there. She rode up to the general store and let her horse drink from the trough. She remained astride for a moment, numb, unsure of what to do next. While riding her only thought had been to get away. Now that she had time to think, she thought maybe she should return to Luke.

Seeing that her horse was spent, she hitched him to the post, wishing she hadn't been so eager to follow Luke's plea to flee. She feared going back home; her father would be so wrathful at her disappearance – and her mother – sure, she would like to see her mother, but her father would not be happy with her. If she were less ladylike she would have cursed. Instead she dismounted and paced in front of the store while her horse continued to drink. Finally, after several people had looked at her strangely as they walked past, she went inside the store.

'Why, Miss Miranda, it isn't time yet for your monthly visit,' said the jovial owner from behind the counter.

'No, it isn't, but I'm here to ask you a favor,' she replied in a halting voice.

'Is there something wrong, my dear?'

'No, there's nothing wrong. Why?'

'You look disheveled – your hair is a mess and you keep looking at the door. Is somebody after you?'

'Oh, Mr Tanner,' she cried, distraught, 'I cannot lie. I am in trouble. There's a man who's after me. I'm so afraid, I don't know what to do.' She was babbling, but she was reluctant to tell Tanner about Luke. Tanner had come out from behind the counter and was now patting her hand.

'There, there, it's all right, Miss Miranda. Let's get you back home where you'll be safe. I can have one of my stock boys ride on to your father's ranch—'

'No! I'm afraid he – the man – might follow me home. I need someplace to stay until I know it's safe.'

Tanner gave her a curious look.

'Why of course, Miss Miranda. You can stay here at my place; Mrs Tanner and the boys should be there, getting supper ready. It's upstairs, this way.' He led her to a back-room from which led a staircase. 'Just knock and let her know the situation. I'll take care of your horse.'

'Thank you, Mr Tanner, thank you so much for your generosity.'

'T'ain't nothing, ma'am. You should calm your nerves with a nice cup of tea until this all blows over.'

Miranda flashed him a warm smile, then went up the stairs. She knocked once on the door at the top and was let in by a woman almost as big as Tanner. Her blonde hair was tied back under a kerchief over her head.

'Come in, dearie. What can I do for you?'

Miranda told Mrs Tanner the same tale she as she had told her husband. Mrs Tanner responded with a sympathetic gesture.

'Oh, those evil men! Always looking to do harm to a pretty young girl. You need to find yourself a right good husband like my William. Say, though, what were you doing out riding alone like that? You should be more careful. Come on, my dear. Would you like some tea? I'll put a kettle on the fire. I'll get one of the boys to . . . Peter, put that down now.'

Miranda was relieved that Mrs Tanner, in her concern for her plight, was so distracted that she didn't have time to question Miranda's story. Like Mr Tanner she had taken it at face value. For now Miranda would stay here, away from the trouble between the Driscolls and her father. Oh! How she wished she could stay until those troubles resolved themselves, then she could marry Luke and have her father walk her down the aisle.

Perhaps that was asking too much, but for now she would stay here until she could think of what to do next.

CHAPTER 8

The journey back from Austin was a long one. Maryanne hadn't been keen on staying with her sister. No, that was an understatement: they had almost been forced to hogtie her to keep her from rejoining Nate. He had been firm though: her safety was paramount. In the end she calmed down when Nate told her he would be back for her.

'I'm worried about the baby. Let me and Luke handle McTavish, and then I'll come back.'

Her sister held her close while Nate and Seamus saddled up and rode out. He resisted the temptation to look back, not trusting himself, knowing the lump in his throat would only grow.

Seamus was quiet while they rode. At first Nate had been grateful for the silence, he could work through his emotions. But now he wanted someone to talk to, to keep his mind off Maryanne and the trouble with McTavish. At last, unable to bear it any longer, he said:

'Good weather, but looks like there's storm clouds a-comin'.'

'Yep, looks like you're right, boss. You reckon your

brother and the rest of them boys got the herd ready? If a storm comes up those beefers will scatter.'

'Don't worry, they'll get the herd to the stockyards. At least as long as McTavish doesn't poke his nose into our business. Let's try to stay ahead of those storm clouds for now.'

'We should make good time to the next town, boss.'

'The sooner the better, before we're drenched.'

To Nate's chagrin the storm clouds followed them. Before they could find shelter a torrential downpour had been unleashed. Having no other choice Nate and Seamus pulled their hats down, wrapped their coats more tightly around themselves and urged their horses on.

Eventually they came to a small town with a saloon. They had passed it on their way east but had not stopped. Now it offered much needed shelter and rest. The two weary travelers put their horses in the stable, getting the ostler to see that their mounts were rubbed down and stocked with oats and fresh water. Then they clomped into the saloon, their soaked gear dripping water as they walked up to the bar.

'Two rooms, please, for one night,' Nate told the stout barkeep.

'Any port in a storm, eh, and you had to come to mine?' was the sour welcome he offered. 'You two are making my nice clean floor all wet.'

Nate glanced down at the dirt and grime and thought he saw a cockroach scurrying away.

'My apologies, sir. If we could have our rooms we will go upstairs and change.'

The barkeep eyed Nate for a long moment. Nate

matched his stare and at last the man blinked.

'It'll be ten dollars for a night – for each of you. That should cover the cleaning charge, too.'

Seamus was about to open his mouth to complain but Nate put his hand up.

'That will be fine. Here's the money.' He threw down two double eagles on the bar. 'We'll be needing food too, and hot baths.'

The barkeep looked at the coins, then his expression softened.

'Why certainly, sir. Anything I can do for you.'

Nate turned around then and saw for the first time that several hard-looking men were sitting down, drinking. Now they were all were looking at him and Seamus. Nate straightened his back and inhaled deeply, his fingers dancing near his revolver.

'Say, mister, you fellows ain't from around here, are ya?' said one swarthy-looking man whose front teeth were missing.

'We're just passing through. Now, if you'll excuse us, my companion and I have to get out of these wet clothes before we further upset the proprietor of this fine establishment.'

'Hold on, son. Ol' Gus won't mind if we have a little chat, will you, Gus? Now let's have us a little parley about those double eagles, shall we?'

Nate glanced back to see that the barkeep, Gus, had disappeared. By the time he looked back 'toothless' was standing up, his hat tilted back, his hands resting on his gunbelt.

'Now maybe I wasn't too clear before, so I'll speak real slow this time. Hand – over – your money, cowboy. *Now*.

'You tell 'em, Tobias!' hollered one of his companions.

'Get that rich fool's money.' Now the tooth-bereft man's other supporters egged him on.

Nate breathed in deeply, thought of Maryanne, his ranch and his new baby. He reached for his belt. He pulled out his wallet and threw it on the floor in front of Tobias.

'There you are, son. Feel free to take as much money as you want. A poor sap like you needs all the money he can get. Why don't you fix your teeth while you're at it?'

Ignoring the insults, Tobias bent over to collect the wallet. That was when Nate's boot hit him square in the mouth, knocking him backward. At the same moment Seamus drew and fired at the crowd of men, who were already reaching for their irons.

Nate did a quick count as he got his own gun unholstered. There were six of them, not including Tobias who was looking for the rest of his teeth on the floor. Seamus's quick draw took two of them out of the action. They writhed on the ground; one had a gaping chest wound, it looked like he was a goner. The other was holding his arm askew as he hid under a table. That left four men standing against two: fair odds for the travelers. Nate got off a shot, then dived behind the bar. The cowardly Gus had disappeared, Nate hadn't seen where he'd gone.

The lead was flying now as the other four scoundrels found their courage. Rows of bottles behind Nate were shattered, shards of glass rained down on him. He wondered what had happened to Seamus. He hoped his ranch hand hadn't been gunned down.

At last the bottle racks were empty and the shower of glass eased off. The men stopped firing to reload.

'Where's the other one? Do you think he's dead?' one of them asked.

Then Nate heard a shot. One of the four men crumpled to the floor.

'Damn! There's the other one. He's got Hank. . . .'

Nate jumped up and fired, gunning down the remaining three surprised desperadoes. He came out from behind the bar and walked over to the still kneeling Tobias. He scooped up his wallet, then lifted Tobias to his feet. He saw Seamus walking towards them.

'Not so courageous now, are you, Tobias?'

'We were only funnin' you, mister. No hard feelings, eh?'

Nate looked around at the carnage.

'Tell that to your *compadres* – the ones who are still alive. Now vamoose before I put a bullet between your eyes.'

The now toothless Tobias, his legs shaking, scampered through the door. At this moment Gus reappeared. Nate turned to him.

'You can add this to our clean-up charge. When you have a moment could you bring the food up to our rooms, please?'

'Yes sir, soon as I can, sir,' the clearly shaken Gus said as Nate, with Seamus following, walked up the stairs.

Nate and Seamus left the saloon as dawn broke. Nate didn't think he'd bother remembering the name of the place, nor did they spend much time taking leave of Gus. Instead they got their now fully rested horses saddled and ready to ride. One quick stop at the general store on the way out of the town saw them supplied for the remainder of the trip. The weather had cleared up after raining through the night. If they made good time, they could be back at the ranch in a couple of days.

After a few hours' riding away from the small town Nate was munching on a stick of jerky when Seamus rode up beside him. He had been trailing behind; now his face was creased with concern.

'Hey boss, I think we're being followed.'

Nate arched one eyebrow. 'You reckon it's Tobias – or his friends?'

Seamus nodded.

'Damn!' Nate cursed. 'I thought we were rid of him. He seemed like the cowardly type. Maybe he's got himself a new bunch of friends. Not good. Looks like we'll have to fight him to get ourselves rid of him. So much for mercy, eh? You got your Winchester ready?'

'I've got ol' Bessy ready to go.' Seamus patted his rifle in its scabbard.

'Sounds good. Now, let's find the high ground and get a little distance between us and them. Once you get a clear shot, don't hesitate.'

Nate dug his spurs into his horse, urging it forward; Seamus was following right behind him. Soon he heard the telltale sound of pounding hoofs coming closer. He couldn't tell how many men were behind them, but more than two was a reasonable assumption.

Nate steered his horse off the path and headed for a patch of undergrowth, Seamus on his heels. Ahead he saw a small rise, a rocky ledge jutting out, surrounded by trees; it seemed good enough cover from which to launch their counter attack. Nate pointed. Seamus nodded and rode ahead so that he could get into position while Nate slowed for his pursuers to catch up.

He didn't have to wait long before five horsemen rode into view. Nate fired his pistol at random and pushed his horse toward the rocky outcrop. There, he hoped, Seamus was lying in wait with his precisely accurate rifle.

Tobias and his cronies started closing fast once they saw Nate shooting at them. Fearless, the lead rider pulled a rifle from his scabbard and got ready to aim on the run. Nate dived from his horse just before the gunman pulled the trigger. He landed on his shoulder while his horse kept galloping toward the rise.

He was still too far away, maybe three hundred yards from the trees, to make it on foot. He just hoped that he was close enough to be within Seamus's range. He scrambled to find any kind of cover in the short grass as a couple of shots came close to hitting him. *Come on*, he willed Seamus, *open fire.*

As if in answer to his thoughts Seamus did start firing on Tobias and his men. He hit one of them dead center in the chest; the rider had been holding the reins with one hand, letting his left arm hang by his side. The rider fell forward over his horse, blood spraying from his open wound.

Narrowing the odds, good, thought Nate.

The others backed away, unsure of where the gunman was.

'Come on, you idiots, there's only two of them, and one of them is unhorsed.' Nate heard the shrill voice of Tobias call out. Nate couldn't resist taunting him.

'You yellow belly. Fight me like a man,' he called out.

The answer he got was gunfire. One of the bullets clipped his leg.

Damn! he thought, *should have kept my big mouth shut.*

Seamus quickly returned fire, keeping the would-be killers at bay. Nate knew his best chance for survival lay in meeting up with his ranch hand. To that end he desperately crawled through the high grass, his leg spilling blood as he went.

Almost there, maybe another hundred yards. Nate dared a peek back. The gunmen were still not moving forward, afraid of Seamus's deadly accuracy. He gritted his teeth as his leg throbbed and redoubled his efforts to meet up with Seamus. There came a pause in the gunfire; Nate suspected that Seamus was reloading but then he heard a shot followed almost immediately by a scream. Nate's heart stuck in his throat. It sounded like Seamus.

He heard war whoops from behind and the steady clomping of horses' hoofs.

Damn! he thought, *maybe they got Seamus.*

Then, as Nate continued to struggle on the ground, four horsemen rode up and surrounded him.

'Well, well, what have we here,' said Tobias through the remains of his broken teeth.

Nate grabbed his pistol and turned over on his back in one motion, thinking to take as many of the riders as he could with him. As he brought his gun up a boot came down hard on his right forearm, pressing his gun flat against the ground. It fired harmlessly into the dirt.

Tobias was standing over him, his rifle slung across his shoulder. The man whose boot was still pressing down on Nate's arm had a gun pointed directly at Nate's head.

'Not going anywhere now, are we, cowboy?'

'You can have my wallet now and leave me in peace to die.'

'Wallet, eh? It's a little too late for that now, *Driscoll.* Nope, your hide is worth more to us alive, cowboy.'

'How do you know my name?' Nate said, then groaned, knowing the answer.

'A sheriff in Garrison has posted a bounty on you and your brother for murder and kidnapping. How much was that for? Five thousand dollars? Two and a half thousand apiece, eh? Now it's a little more, now that poor ol' Ted got filled with lead. Hey, that rhymes. Anyway, we didn't know nothing about you being Driscoll until right now, when you just confirmed it. Lucky guess on my part. Your friend is no use to us, unless he's your brother.'

Nate didn't know what to say; he just nodded slowly.

'Find out if the other one is still alive, and whether he's a Driscoll,' Tobias said over his shoulder. 'If he ain't a Driscoll put a bullet in him.'

Nate tried to move to get a shot off, to get away from this malevolent, evil man, but one silent signal from Tobias put an end to his struggles. Two men took his gun away and bound his hands tightly behind his back. The third man came riding back from the ridge.

'The man's dead. Clay got him with one shot.'

'Too bad. If he was your brother we don't get to collect that reward. No matter – one Driscoll's good enough. Let's go, boys.'

'It's hard to lift him up. His leg is dragging.'

'Here, give him this for the pain.' Tobias came over and lifted Nate's head by the hair.

The last image Nate saw was the butt of Tobias's pistol slamming into his face.

CHAPTER 9

Luke watched the gunman until he was a speck on the horizon. He let out the breath he hadn't realized he was holding and walked back to his men.

'Jim Tucker's dead, expired from his wounds. What's the plan now?' asked Taggart, quietly.

Luke surveyed his group of hands and didn't answer right away. There were only four men left. Five if he counted himself; not enough to run the herd up to Kansas.

'Everybody, listen up. This is what we're going to do. I promised my brother we would take his herd to Kansas, but we can't go back to the ranch on account of us probably being wanted men. Miss Miranda is safe in the town and will probably find her way back to her father's ranch. Still, given his unforgiving nature, I doubt that we will be exonerated. So we have to round up as much of the herd as we can and drive them to the trail-drive gathering in Austin. We'll have to pay a trail boss to take them from there to Abilene.'

'How do you intend to get at the herd? They're still scattered all over the spread,' asked Doug.

'We'll gather as many as we can. Doug, you'll take the rest of the men and come around the southern tip of the ranch. There were a bunch of straggling beefers there. Herd as many as you can manage – maybe one or two hundred – and then meet me north of town, by the chimney rock, in two days.'

'Where are you going?'

'To cause a distraction so you can get in and out of our spread without being molested.'

Luke mounted his horse. His plan was only half-formed in his brain, but he was too scared to back down.

'If I'm not back soon leave without me. Drive the herd to Austin. I'll meet you there.'

With that he waved at his still gawping ranch hands, and rode toward town, leaving behind his men with a half-empty wagon to puzzle out their own plan for driving the cattle to the trail-drive meeting point.

Luke kept riding on past the town. He wanted to remain hidden so he headed straight for the McTavish ranch. He was working out a plan of action on the fly, and was becoming desperate. But desperate men were unpredictable, and this was what Luke wanted to drill home to McTavish: that Luke Driscoll was unpredictable – and dangerous.

He skirted the edge of McTavish's property, looking for any scouting riders. Seeing none, he dismounted near a dry gully. He hid his saddle and tack behind a large boulder and let his horse roam free. There was plenty of grass and a water source, if it rained, which looked likely.

After checking his ammo and making sure that both

his rifle and his pistol were loaded he climbed out of the gully and on to a rocky ledge. He kept walking until the ledge began to rise again. There was a rocky outcrop, hidden among the trees, which overlooked the McTavish land. Luke had noticed it before on one of his scouting trips along the land boundary, and had marked it in his mind as a good place to lay an ambush. Luke settled into a cranny in the rocks and waited. He wished he had some men and more ammo.

He didn't have long to wait. As the sun was setting a group of riders rode into Luke's line of sight. They wore bandannas marking them as McTavish men. *Four of them, easy pickings*, thought Luke as he raised his rifle. The first shot took the lead rider out before he could even turn his head. It took a split second for the other riders to react; in that time Luke had gunned another one down. The remaining two went into a panic. They started shooting at random: then, after a third shot from Luke sailed over their heads, they spurred their horses toward the home-stead, galloping as fast as they could.

Luke smiled to himself. That should have provided the necessary distraction, he thought. McTavish would send men here to find him. As he wondered whether he should stay where he was and wait for those men or move on to another ambush site the rain began to fall. His dilemma temporarily solved, he hunkered down to wait out the storm.

As he munched on hard biscuits left over from his trail pack his thoughts wandered to Miranda. He hoped she was safe but, thinking that likely, he hoped even more that a rift hadn't developed between them. It would be a hell of a thing to ask a woman to choose between a man and her family. He didn't want it to come down to that. Damn that McTavish! If he hadn't been so greedy, this all could have been avoided. As the rain pelted the makeshift shelter provided by his poncho, which he'd strung between branches of the trees, Luke drifted off to sleep.

He awoke to loud voices shouting to each other. The rain had stopped. Luke checked his weapons to make sure that no water had got into them, and steadied himself. There were at least twenty men now spreading out in front of him, several carrying torches. Fire appeared to be one of McTavish's favorite weapons. It was effective, Luke had to admit. The one attack he couldn't defend himself against was a brush fire. He would be smoked out and ridden to ground. At least, that would be McTavish's plan. Before that happened he would take as many of McTavish's men as he could.

Luke let loose a shot that forced the advancing men to pull back. Luke knew he was outgunned: once they got close enough the men would drop their torches. He was lucky that it had rained heavily; with the ground so wet the fire would be slow to spread, though the smoke would obscure his vision.

He fired off another round from his rifle, then ran down behind the outcrop of rocks. He had thought to double back and get his horse, then he remembered that he had hidden his saddle. It would take too much time to find his horse and saddle it. So instead he made a break for it, running as fast as he could. Hearing shots fired didn't cause him to pause, Luke's lungs were on fire, but he knew stopping would bring death. Soon the pungent smell of burning wood came to his nose; risking a backward glance he saw a column of black smoke rising slowly into the sky. Shaking his head at McTavish's desperation he pressed on, hoping to keep one step ahead of his pursuers.

CHAPTER 10

Miranda listened to the rain pattering heavily on the roof. It was so loud she couldn't sleep. She paced around the small bedroom the Tanners had provided for her, worrying about Luke. At last, the rain slackened off and she fell asleep, still with no idea of how she was going to extricate herself from the mess she now found herself in. If suspicions were ever aroused in her father's mind he would end any budding romance between her and the Driscoll brother. The longer she could avoid that confrontation the better, she told herself. She could only hope that the truth would not occur to him.

That morning she sat down to breakfast with Mrs Tanner and the two boys.

'Where is Mr Tanner?' she asked after she had helped herself to a plateful of bacon and grits.

'Mr Tanner had to leave early this morning. He has to see to a shipment that is coming in today. With the terrible storm last night he wanted to make sure the wagons have made it safely.'

Miranda was continuing to eat her breakfast in silence when suddenly she heard booted footsteps outside on the landing. She assumed it was Mr Tanner coming back, but it sounded as if there was more than one person. At that moment Mrs Tanner and her two boys rushed into the kitchen. Miranda gasped as the door swung open to reveal her father and four of his men.

'I'm sorry, Miss McTavish, but I thought it would be best to contact your father, seeing as you were worried about some strange men following you,' Mr Tanner said, stepping out from behind her father. He came toward her. 'I'm only a humble shopkeeper. I cannot offer protection.' The man seemed apologetic as he wrung his hat in his hands.

'I see, Mr Tanner. Well, that is no problem. You did the right thing. Hello, Father.'

'Miranda, thank God you're safe! Your mother and I have been frantic in searching for you. We've been so worried. Was it the Driscolls? Did they kidnap you?'

'No, Father, no one kidnapped me. I only went out for a ride and was caught in a Comanche ambush. Luke – Mr Driscoll – saved my life and I—'

McTavish waved his hand to cut her short.

'Tut-tut, my dear, you're not yourself. We can talk more when we get you back home. Mr Tanner, thank you for leading me to my daughter. You say you didn't see anyone else with her?'

'No, Mr McTavish, she only said that some strange man was following her.'

'That's fine. It was wise of you to tell me. Now come, Miranda, we have a horse waiting for you.'

Miranda's eyes were wide with fear, then she slowly resigned herself to her fate.

'Yes, Father, we should go home.' She eyed the men

who were standing round her in a semicircle, all with their hands hitched along their gunbelts, all staring at her. They fell in behind her as she stepped forward. Once they were all outside she saw that there were two more men waiting; one was holding the reins of her recently saddled horse.

'Up you go, darling.' Her father's face wore a cheery smile; she had forgotten how nice he could be. His easy demeanour reassured her. Perhaps things would not be as bad as she had thought.

The ride home was quiet, though her father's men kept giving furtive glances in every direction.

'There's been more than a few incidents with the Driscolls. That's why we have all the extra protection,' McTavish told her. 'You'll be safe enough in the ranch house with your ma and sisters.'

'I hope so, Father, I surely hope so.' She worried now about what sort of incidents involved Luke.

Back at home Miranda was greeted warmly by her mother and two younger sisters. They bustled her into the house while her father sat his horse, pointedly watching her. Miranda, despite her father's gentle treatment of her, was still too afraid to speak of her feelings about Luke. Maybe later, she thought.

As her sister closed the door she risked one last look at her father. He was still staring at her, but now his eyes had grown hard, and his lips, no longer smiling, were set straight and stern.

He knows, Miranda thought, *Oh no! This is going wrong*.

Her stomach felt hollow. Her father knew that she loved Luke and had left with him. For the first time in her life she began to truly fear her father.

*

Luke tried to reach his horse but his pursuers were relentless. He pressed on, finding what little cover he could, taking potshots at the riders. Now and then they would seem to back off, maybe giving him enough time to escape. This happened four or five times, but now Luke was running low on bullets. He knew what they were doing: trying to herd him as if he were a maverick, trying to wear him down. Once he was out of ammo, or simply too exhausted to go on they would pounce.

Luke needed to change the situation and fast. By now his men should have rounded up as many cattle as they could out of the Driscoll range and would be headed for Austin. He was continuing south, already on his brother's lands. He needed a horse badly and was hoping there were still a few strays left around the stables. Luke knew they hadn't taken all of them when they left. McTavish's men might anticipate his moves – might already have coralled the remaining horses.

Seeing an opportunity he ducked behind a large oak tree. He was familiar with this tree, growing near enough to the ranch house for him to be able to see it from the branches. Sweaty after his brief climb he peered into the distance. His worst fears were confirmed: his brother's ranch house had been burned to ashes. Nothing he could do about it now, Luke was more concerned about the stables. Looking beyond the ruins of the ranch he could see that building still standing.

Good, he thought, that means there are still horses there. He estimated the distance to be about two hundred yards, ten minutes and he'd be there. Saddle up a horse, make the rendezvous in time, that was the plan. A quick look north showed him the pursuit had slowed, there was no sign of the riders. Luke could hear their voices carrying in the distance, growing faint. He blessed his luck; they were headed the wrong way. He dropped his trail pack on the ground and burst into a run. He was exposed over this open ground so the sooner he got to the stables the better.

His lungs were burning halfway there when he heard a shout from behind. Damn, he'd been spotted. No hope for it now, he had to get on a horse or he was a dead man. He reached the stables out of breath, but his eyes lit up when he saw six horses stabled there. So that was why McTavish left the stables alone: his men were using them. *Lucky me*, thought Luke, now to get a saddle. Hastily he saddled up the nearest horse. As he cinched the saddle tight, he could hear the voices of his would-be captors outside. He jumped on the horse and urged it to kick the now unlocked stable doors. As he came into the open shots whizzed past him. He pulled on the reins, turned the horse and dug his boots into its flanks.

Taking off at a gallop, he stayed ahead of McTavish's men. His horse was fresh, well rested, and soon they left the tired, spent mounts of the outriders behind. By doubling back and leaving a false trail Luke was confident that he would meet up with his men and the cattle.

Breathing easier, the adrenaline still coursing through his veins he allowed himself a small smile. *This thinking spontaneously does work*, he thought to himself. Nate would hate it though; he was methodical where Luke was impulsive, part of the reason they had had their falling out.

That should be ancient history now that his brother

had Maryanne, and soon he might have Miranda, at least, so he hoped. Both brothers, once fighting over a woman, now ending up with two women whose names begin with M. He mused over that symmetry for a while. As twilight began to settle in Luke's stomach began to growl. A quick stop to let his horse rest and him to find some grub would still allow enough time to meet the boys. Even if he missed them he could easily catch up with them on the trail.

So, Luke stopped behind a group of boulders and turned the horse loose to graze while he hunted for game. There was no sign of pursuit so he built a small fire and cooked the two rabbits he had shot. After eating he closed his eyes, not realizing how tired he had been; a quick catnap and he'd be ready for the trail again, he told himself as he drifted off to sleep.

CHAPTER 11

When Nate came to, he found himself tied to the back end of a mule. He was still groggy but the uneven gait of the mule had jostled him awake. Raising his head he saw Tobias, leading the group. Going by the position of the sun, they appeared to be heading south, toward Garrison and his ranch. Nate felt a hard blow in the back of his head, causing him to tear up instinctively but not pass out.

'Why don't you take another nap, cowboy.' The speaker, one of Tobias's ruffians, leered at him and raised the butt of his rifle for another strike. Nate braced himself, then the mule suddenly stumbled, lurched, and Nate fell to the ground.

The man's rifle hit the mule's rump off which Nate had fallen. The mule responded by viciously kicking out, clipping the man's horse. This caused the horse to buck, throwing the rider, who twisted in the air and landed on his side, totally winded. Nate saw his chance; desperately he abraded the thin rope against a rock to free his hands. The outlaw stumbled to his feet, dazed after his fall, and his fellows were now turning around to see what the commotion was.

Fortunately Nate had been next to last in the column and the unhorsed bandit was the rearguard.

With a snap the rope broke and Nate's hands were free. He double-fisted his hands and brought them straight down on the unhorsed man, who was still staggering on his feet. The two men struggled to gain leverage as Nate fought with hands that were numb from restricted blood flow. If he could only get his captor's gun he might have a chance.

Too late: Tobias and the other three men were now coming back to assist their comrade.

'Come on, Jeffro, don't let a bound man get the best of you,' said the ringleader.

'He's as strong as a polecat, boss, even with . . . pah.' Nate socked the man in the mouth, double-fisted, disorienting him. Nate had his chance now, with the man's arms flailing; he made a grab for Jeffro's gun, had got it halfway out of the holster when a shot landed at his feet, sending dirt flying upward.

'That's enough horsing around. I'll bring you in dead if I have to. Earn your pay, Jeffro, and keep a better eye on our prisoner, or I'll replace you.' Tobias leered at Jeffro as he spoke, causing the other man to shrink back.

This man, Tobias, is nothing more than a bully, thought Nate. *Perhaps I can use that to my advantage.* Nate stood still as Jeffro retied his bonds.

'So, Jeffro is it?'

'Yup, that's my name, cowboy. What of it?'

'Only wondering if you're the same Jeffro what held up the National Bank in San Antonio. Jeffro Longmont, was it? What gang were you with then?'

'I don't know what you're talking about, mister.'

'Quit gabbing and let's go, we've got a meeting to make,' yelled Tobias. Jeffro retied the knots and placed Nate back on the mule. Sweaty with the exertion, he remounted his grazing horse and took the lead of the mule. Nate was unfazed as they continued on.

'It's just that if you are the same Jeffro as robbed the San Antonio bank and took a potshot at the sheriff, why do you let anyone boss you around? Least of all a pussy-willow like Tobias. Or maybe I'm thinking of a different Jeffro. If so, my apologies; please carry on.'

Jeffro didn't reply but Nate could see the man grit his teeth. Maybe he had hit on something here; it could help him out of the jam he was in. He hoped. He tried one more time, 'So that bounty on me, is it real? Or is it McTavish's doing?'

'You don't know when to quit, do ya? Hey, Clay, what's the remedy for a too talkative captive?'

The rider in front turned his head, gave a wry smile.

'Back in the war we used to cut out their tongues,' he said. 'Stopped them talking real quick.'

Jeffro gave Nate a pointed look, and the rancher fell silent. This was going to be harder than he'd thought.

Luke watched the riders ahead of him warily. They had passed him unawares in the night. It was lucky they hadn't seen him since Luke hadn't woken up until dawn. The lack of a fire had probably helped to keep him unseen. Now, though, he had a clear view of them. They were far to the north of Garrison; he had already passed the rendezvous point with no sign of the Driscoll ranch hands or any cattle. He hoped his men hadn't bugged out on him altogether, that they simply hadn't waited for him for very long.

Worried about McTavish's men doubling back, he kept heading north. Perhaps he'll meet up with the men or even Nate, thought Luke. Growing more apprehensive the longer he traveled with no sight of the drovers or beefers, Luke started to wonder whether he shouldn't go back to the family spread.

He continued on until the end of the day, but his optimism waned. That night, now miles away from Garrison, he set camp. There was no one on the trail, not his men, not McTavish's men, not strangers, no one. Luke began to wonder sardonically whether he hadn't taken a wrong turn somewhere.

Shrugging off his concerns, he went to hunt for his dinner. His ammunition was low, so every shot counted. If he missed he might go hungry. He was lucky tonight, though, as he bagged two jackrabbits, enough meat to last a few days. If he didn't find his men soon, however, he'd have to turn back; he didn't think he had enough supplies to last him until Abilene, and even the nearest town was too far away.

That night he slept fitfully, with only his horse to keep him company. The next morning Luke skipped breakfast, resolved to either find the ranch hands or turn back. By midday, after riding through nothing but unbroken wilderness, he was ready to give up.

Then he heard something.

Fearing an ambush Luke looked for cover. He espied, off in the distance, some small of bushes clustered along a shallow ravine. He spurred his horse, hoping to make it there before whoever he'd heard came into view. As he was about to settle into the ravine, keeping his horse carefully screened by the bushes, a group of horsemen came riding from the north. He counted four mounted men, and a mule carrying what looked like a prisoner. Luke edged closer to the trail to get a better look. The prisoner raised his head just as the mule passed Luke's hiding-place.

Luke's heart caught in his throat: it was Nate.

Instinctively Luke reached for his rifle; there were only four of them. He could take them out and rescue his brother. Luke didn't see Seamus, so he was either dead or separated from Nate.

Four against one, he could do it.

Luke almost slammed his rifle in frustration when he saw he only had three cartridges left. His pistol was empty. He couldn't fight the men now, but he could follow them and hope to set his brother free when an opportunity presented itself. The herd and ranch hands were forgotten: Luke only wanted to be reunited with Nate.

His brother's captors seemed slack, lackadaisical; their movements were slow; they'd be easy pickings once they'd camped for the night. Luke waited until he could barely hear them in the distance. They were loud, this lot, so they must be far ahead of him, Luke judged, when eventually he set off to follow them.

Luke soon caught up to them. In fact, he'd had to slow up so they wouldn't sight him if he got too close.

They seemed to be in no hurry, for they stopped to camp a few hours before sundown. Luke stood off in the distance, still ahorse, but, to them, barely a speck on the horizon. His eagle eyes could barely make out their forms. One man, maybe the leader, rode on ahead while the other three built a fire-pit and prepared their bedding. Nate was handled roughly, thrown to the ground and kicked. Luke instinctively caressed his rifle butt, eager to exact vengeance.

As dusk began to set he moved closer to the camp. The man who had left returned with another horseman. So that was why they'd stopped so early: they'd been waiting for someone. Maybe these were McTavish's men and they meant to deliver Nate to him? Luke had been hoping to strike tonight but the arrival of the extra man gave him pause.

Luke got as close as he dared with his horse, then crawled through the grass. In the dim light he could barely make out the men; then, for the second time that day, his heart nearly jumped into his throat. The new arrival to the camp was familiar to Luke. The cocky gait, the way he carried his pistols on his belt: it was the gun-slinger, Beaufort. *Damn! so the plot thickens even more,* thought Luke. He needed to get his brother to safety fast, but Beaufort's presence complicated matters even more for him.

Reluctantly Luke backed away from the camp. As he crawled backwards his left foot hit a big rock causing him to whimper involuntarily in pain. He covered his mouth quickly and put his head in the dirt. Too late, he'd been heard.

'What was that? You hear that noise?'

'Probably a coyote, Dave. Still, it wouldn't hurt to check it out. Could be Comanches.'

'Thanks for the encouragement, Tobias. Hand me

that Henry repeater, just in case.'

Luke didn't dare move as Dave left the camp and headed straight towards him. The new-fledged cowboy had one more ploy in mind in case he was discovered; he fingered his hunting knife strapped to his belt. It had been given to him by an old one-time fur-trapper for whom he'd done a favor in Montana; it had been useful in skinning rabbits and other game he'd got used to catching on his long journey from Montana; now he could take out the outlaw once he got close. Luke made to grab for his knife as the man got closer. Luckily the grass was tall here, after the constant rain, and it was almost dark. The outlaw stopped about three feet from Luke, peering into the distance. Then, muttering to himself, he traced his steps back to the camp.

'You're right,' Luke heard him say. 'It's only a coyote. I didn't see anything out there.'

'All right, Dave. You can help skin these rabbits, then, and make sure the prisoner gets his share. We want him nice and healthy when he meets the boss.'

The rest of the conversation trailed off as Luke continued backing away from the camp. At last he was far enough away, and the light from the sun completely gone, for him to risk standing up. He hurried back to his horse and decided to make his own camp. He still had no plan for rescuing his brother, other than to wait, watch, and follow. When the first opportunity came he would strike and rescue Nate.

He just didn't know when that would be.

CHAPTER 12

Nate ate his food quietly. He was set apart from the men, once again bound hand and foot. His bonds had been loosened now to allow him to eat. This gave him a chance to observe his captors. The new man, called Beaufort by Tobias, seemed to be the leader. At least, he bossed Tobias and the others around as though he were. There was something about him that made Nate nervous. He was too cool and calm, he carried himself like a professional. Where Tobias was all hat and no cattle, a loud braggart, cowardly and easy to put on the floor, this man promised death in his eyes.

Nate lowered his eyes as Tobias came over to him.

'Eat up, dog. This is the last food you're gonna get until you see the boss.' Tobias kicked him. Nate stifled the groan, not wanting to give this man any satisfaction.

'Now, now Tobias, let's treat our prisoner with respect. After all he's worth quite a bit of money,' Beaufort said as he appeared behind Tobias.

'Taking me to the sheriff, eh, for the reward?' Nate goaded him.

'Sheriff? Ha, that bumbling buffoon. No, my dear rancher, you are the ultimate prize for our employer. I'm sure you can figure out who that is. Once you are in his hands, your little land dispute will be over.'

Nate took a deep breath. He'd figured it out long ago that these men had been hired by McTavish. Damn, but that man was evil! He would have to deal with McTavish once and for all – once he was free.

Beaufort turned to leave, but before he moved away he said over his shoulder,

'Oh, by the way, rancher, I ran into your brother. Twice actually; the second time wasn't as friendly a meeting as the first. The third time I meet him he will die.'

The gunslinger said it so matter-of-factly that Nate knew he spoke the truth. *Luke*, Nate thought, now unconcerned for himself, *be careful around this man.*

When Beaufort had left Tobias leaned in close to Nate's face. He could smell the man's rancid breath.

'If I get my way I'll be the one to string you up,' he muttered. 'Looking forward to seeing you swing.' Tobias gave Nate one more kick before he too disappeared into the shadows.

Nate knew what would happen next if he didn't get clear of these ruffians. As the fire burned lower his captors eventually drifted off into sleep. One man, Dave tonight, would be set to watch him. When Dave did eventually come over, he sat next to Nate, not saying anything. Nate pretended to sleep and soon even Dave was snoozing.

Moving slowly to avoid waking Dave up, Nate felt around on the ground for a sharp rock or stick: anything he could use to cut his bonds with. After a bit he found a stone with sharp edges; carefully he slipped it into his back pocket. His bonds would be checked in the morning so there would be no use in trying to cut himself free tonight. Luckily, his pockets hadn't been searched after his capture; he could loosen his bonds gradually and when the men went to sleep he could escape. It would have to be soon as in one more day they would be near Garrison and McTavish. Nate had something now that he hadn't had before: hope and a plan.

Luke watched as the outlaws broke camp. They were heading south and there was little doubt in his mind that they planned on delivering Nate to McTavish. Before that happened Luke had to rescue him.

He shadowed the party as they traveled, making sure to keep his distance. If he was spotted and captured or killed, that would seal Nate's fate. As the day wore on he began to get desperate. He took to riding in a little closer, then slipping back out of possble view. He didn't want to risk the outlaws seeing him, particularly after one of the men started acting as a rearguard, hanging back from the group.

Luke cursed himself for his carelessness and strove to stay further out of sight. Too late; the detached rider mimicked his moves and soon Luke realized that his tactics had been spotted and that he was being played along. He kept a steady distance to see if the man would follow suit. To his horror he turned and came towards him, closing the distance between them fast, his horse breaking into a gallop. Luke turned and spurred his own horse away. Drawing on the fly, he shot wildly behind his back. His pursuer wasn't yet close, but it was enough to make him back off. Luke knew his horse would tire soon; taking a gamble he leapt, landing heavily on his shoulder.

His horse kept going for a bit, in the dim light fooling his pursuer, who kept chasing the now riderless steed.

Too late the pursuer realized his mistake, having passed where Luke was lying on the ground. Two shots startled his horse, which reared up, throwing him. Luke, his shoulder painfully bruised, was on the man before he could stand up, holding his drawn hunting knife to his throat.

'Now, good sir,' Luke said through gritted teeth, 'you're going to tell me everything you know about yonder riders, and everything they know about me.'

The man, lying on his back, licked his chapped lips.

'Whatever you say, chief.'

Luke kept the knife close to the man's throat and listened closely while he spoke. He said his name was Dave. There were five men in total, including one man who had joined them that evening; Dave didn't know his name. Tobias was the boss, they were bounty hunters, ex-rebs now disenfranchised. Tobias had got wind of a job from a rich rancher, who had placed a bounty on a rival. They came across him by happenstance on their way south. Tobias got a boot in his mouth for his trouble. Now they had him and were ready to deliver their captive to the rancher. Tobias had noticed that someone was following them so Dave was sent to chase him off.

Luke relaxed his grip on the knife. Five against one, with one of them likely to be Beaufort, the gunslinger.

'Thank you, Dave,' he said. 'I appreciate the information. I shan't forget to tell Tobias when I see him how you sang.'

Dave spat; Luke, taken by surprise, slowly wiped the spittle from his face.

'Now,' he said, 'to deal with you.' Luke whipped out his gun; Dave's face went white. 'Calm down, I ain't gonna shoot ya. Not yet, at least,' Luke assured him. In one motion Luke flipped his gun around and smashed the butt against the man's skull. Out cold the hired gunman hung limp on Luke's arm.

Acting quickly Luke bound the unconscious Dave's hands then he picked up the man's hat from the ground where it had fallen when Dave was thrown from his horse, he also took the man's bandanna, and jacket. He mounted the gunman's horse, securing his own with a lead and slowly rode to the camp.

As he rode in Luke kept his head down, Dave's hat, a tight fit, was crammed as low over his brow as it would go, the bandanna was wrapped around his mouth. If he caught them unawares his gambit would have a chance. A risk, he knew, but he was always one to take a risk. He could see that all was quiet. A single fire still smoldered in the dark. There was movement to his left. Luke froze.

'Did you get him?' a harsh voice called out.

Luke gave a brisk nod and pointed to his own horse.

'Huh, that's one less barrel-boarder to worry about. Got his horse too. Nice work, Davey.'

Luke continued to ride, acting as nonchalant as he could. Then he heard the click of a hammer pulling back.

Nice try. Very clever using a bandanna, but Dave had long brown hair not short blond hair.' Luke whirled around, bringing to bear his own pistol that he'd carried hidden under his jacket. Firing rapidly he caught the other man off guard. The gunfire woke the others before the sentry had hollered. Luke spurred his horse, leaping over the dying fire.

'Nate! Nate, where are you?' he yelled as the bounty hunters scrambled to their feet.

'Here, Luke.' he heard his brother call, and he almost wept with joy. Nate was at the other end of the camp; Luke could see him, his hands were tied behind his back. Luke urged his mount on, evading the angry grappling hands of the renegade bounty hunters. He pulled hard back on the reins, forcing his horse to rear right in front of Nate's guard. The man collapsed, quailing, his hands covering his head from the lethal hoofs.

'Quick, give me your arm.' Luke grabbed at his brother's crocked elbow, hauling him with all his strength on to the horse. Sitting crosswise along the saddle Nate looked up and gave a weak grin.

'Hullo, Luke. What are you doing here?'

'Getting the hell out of Dodge. Hold on!' He spurred the stallion one more time and, still holding the lead for his own horse, rode hard and fast, away from the outlaw bounty hunters.

CHAPTER 13

Luke looked down on his brother as he slept fitfully, his brow furrowed with worry. A bullet had grazed Nate's leg in the escape. Luke had mended it as best he could and stanched the blood flow, but the wound would slow them down. Reckless, Nate would call him if he was awake. But recklessness had saved Nate. Now the only thing to do was to keep ahead of the bounty hunters and get Nate to a doctor: easy enough. Luke wished he was as confident as he sounded. He knew there were still five violent and dangerous men hunting them.

Nate slowly stirred on the ground.

'Good, you're awake. We've got to ride. McTavish's men are coming,' Luke told him.

'I know. Hold on, help me up.'

'You can ride Dave's horse.'

'How far back are they, you think?'

Luke peered into the distance. 'I don't know. We got away quick, then I laid a false trail. I don't see any dust cloud behind us. With any luck they'll have followed it. But they won't be fooled for long and you're still hurt.'

Nate nodded, 'Let's get moving. Don't worry about my

leg, he just winged me. We going back to the Bar D?'

'Been meaning to tell you about that. Things went from bad to worse when you left. The ranch house got burned down. McTavish's doing. The herd's lost, and the hands have scattered to the four winds – if they're not dead.'

'Last time I leave you in charge, little brother. Maryanne is safe in Austin. Let's go there, get my wife and bring the Rangers down on McTavish. He's gone too far.' Luke couldn't disagree with his brother. This feud had got beyond them; they needed help or McTavish would bury them both.

It was slow going as Luke tried to get their bearings. In the helter-skelter dash out of the bounty hunter camp last night he hadn't picked a direction. His one thought had been to flee. Now he wished he had been more methodical in his escape.

Checking the sun Luke concluded that they had moved west. They were in some badlands: unfamiliar territory. He wanted to go north and east to get to Maryanne, but west first was desirable, then doubling back to string out their pursuers.

Once he'd secured his brother on his horse Luke saddled Dave's roan stallion and got ready to ride. He risked a glance back and saw a billowing cloud of dust in the distance. The bounty hunters had found them.

'Come on, Nate, we've got to haul ass. Find cover, quick.'

'Right. Luke. Let's go. You got an extra iron for me?'

'Here, use Dave's.' He tossed Nate a .44.

'Let's go. Yeehaa!' He spurred his mount and rode to a gallop, giving one more backward glance to make sure that his brother was following right behind him.

*

Miranda was kept in her room for the next couple days. Her father would see her occasionally but it was mostly her mother, Linda, and her two younger sisters who spent time with her. To keep her mind busy she knitted and helped her mom with the cooking. Though she was allowed to move freely about the house and even outside, there was always one of the ranch hands near by, watching her closely without seeming to. Her father either didn't trust Miranda or was worried that she would wander off again; whichever it was the instruction was clear: Miranda wasn't to leave the house without permission or a heavy escort.

Two days after her return home a rider came to the ranch, one of her father's punchers, who quickly sought out the ranch owner. In hushed and hurried tones they talked behind closed doors in her father's study. Miranda resisted the urge to eavesdrop and soon her father and the rider came out of the study. The rider quickly left while her father, his face flushed and his eyes restless, called for his foreman. When he came McTavish told him:

'Zack, bring more men. We've got 'em. The bounty hunters worked well. They're north of us. That man I hired—' the rest of his response came to an abrupt stop as the two men went into the study and closed the door, but Miranda, hidden in a nook that she was pretending to clean, had heard enough. Luke and his brother were caught and her father was going to them, perhaps to string them up.

Her face went pale at the thought. She knew she had

97

to go to Luke, to help him as much as possible. Her father had become mad; he wouldn't listen to reason. No, it would tear her family apart. Now she was conflicted. Slowly she walked to her room. Her mother was there, straightening her sheets.

'Miranda, sweetie, what's wrong with you? You look like you've seen a ghost.'

'Oh, Mama, I think I'm in trouble.'

'Please, dear, tell me all about it.'

'I'm in love, Mama, but it's with a man who could tear our family apart.'

In desperation she told her mother everything about Luke Driscoll and what her father had done. Her mother listened with sympathetic attention, holding her hand.

'Oh dear,' she said as Miranda finished. 'I had no idea. Sure, I had an inkling that there was something bothering you, but not on this scale.' She sighed.

'Don't tell Papa, there's no telling what he'll do.'

'Your father has changed, that's for sure. This war with the Driscolls, it's changed him, he's obsessed. But sweetie, you mustn't worry about him; you have to follow your heart. Your sisters and I will help you. Here's what we'll do.'

As Miranda listened to her mother's plan her heart pounded in excitement, and she couldn't suppress the wide grin that appeared on her face. Soon she would be with Luke, her father be damned.

The pain in Nate's leg still throbbed as they raced away from the gunmen, but the circulation had returned to his hands after being bound for so long. At least that was something. He was tempted to tell Luke to leave him behind, but knew it would be futile. His younger brother would refuse, stubborn as ever, and force him to come along. He could appreciate that sentiment. In fact he owed his brother his life. It was quite a turn-around for their relationship. Nate wouldn't have bothered sending for his brother if it had not been for his desperate situation. Now he was thankful for Luke's presence. If they got out of this mess alive and stopped McTavish, then it would be worth it.

Luke kept up a furious pace and Nate was afraid of blacking out. They were short on water and food but Nate knew they'd be caught if they stopped. It was noon before Luke called a halt, he'd found a rock formation that offered shelter, and grass near by for the horses to graze. Nate was glad for the respite, the pain in his leg was still there, now a dull throb. He was afraid to put any weight on it, fearing his leg would collapse under him. After Luke had unsaddled his horse he went to help Nate.

Nate touched the ground gingerly. Reluctantly he put weight on his right leg, the one that had been shot. He let out a sigh of relief when the leg didn't buckle under him. Waving his brother off, Nate limped to a rocky outcrop to sit down, grimacing as he did so.

'Any better?' his brother asked.

'No, but I think it will be. The bleeding's stopped but the bullet may still be in there.'

'Let's see what we can do about that. If it stays in there any longer the wound'll get infected.' Nate gave his brother a hard look as Luke brandished his hunting knife. He lit a match under it and carefully drew it along the edge of the blade.

'Take off your britches. I think we've got a little time.'

'You know what you're doing, little brother?'

'Not really, but I don't think we have any other choice.'

Grudgingly Nate agreed and removed his trousers. He flinched at the sight of the wound; it was worse than he'd thought. It was more than a flesh wound, the bullet hadn't grazed him but had gouged a big hole in his leg.

'Guess I was more hurt than I thought,' he said meekly as Luke motioned for him to lie down.

'I don't have any whiskey, so you'll have to grit your teeth hard. Have you got anything to bite down on? Ah, your belt. Good. Ready . . . three . . two . . .' At two Luke plunged his heated knife into the wound. Nate stifled a scream by biting down hard on his leather belt. It felt like an eternity before Luke stood up and shoved something under Nate's eyes.

'Look at that. One .44 bullet safely removed. I've got a bit of thread I can sew you up with. Pretty crude but it will do until we get you to a doctor.'

'Not bad for a gold prospector. Thanks, little brother.' Nate managed a weak smile as Luke finished his ministrations.

'Any time. When the horses finish eating and are rested up we'll head out again. I'll keep watch if you want to nap.'

Nate nodded, acknowledging how weak and tired he felt. Before long his eyelids became heavy and he couldn't help falling asleep.

Nate awoke to the sound of gunshots. Cursing, he groped around for his gun, then realized he hadn't put on his pants. Jumping up, he found that his leg was still painful, but he dressed quickly and buckled his gunbelt, putting his .44 in his hand. He came around to the front of the rock formation to see his brother dragging a jackrabbit along the ground.

'Damnation, Luke! Why don't you warn someone before you go shooting rabbits? I thought them damned bounty hunters were on us.'

'Sorry, Nate. Didn't want to wake you. Anyway, I got dinner.'

'Thanks, Luke. Say, where do you reckon those bounty hunters are? I thought they were right behind us.'

'Don't know. I thought that dust cloud was them, but I haven't seen hide nor hair of them. It's got me worried. My false trail wasn't that good, they could find us. For now, let's not curse our good luck; we can eat and double back and get to Austin that much sooner.'

'Sounds good, Luke, I'll help you with that rabbit.'

Luke was cheerful as he skinned the dead rabbit and Nate built the fire. But Nate couldn't help but worry that they were being set up. McTavish wasn't likely to give up and he was sure that Tobias and his cronies wouldn't stop until he was recaptured.

CHAPTER 14

They slept that night amongst the rocky outcroppings, far from any civilization. Luke woke early, still fearing that Beaufort and his gunmen were after them. After a quick breakfast of leftover rabbit Luke helped his brother into his saddle and the two rode west for a short time. Even though he had patched Nate up as best he could Luke feared his brother had lost too much blood. His face was still pale, pale enough to suggest that he needed to see a doctor, or at least have bedrest. His brother's health and their lack of water – only half a canteen left – made the decision easy. After a few miles Luke held up his hand.

'Time to double back and pray that McTavish's men aren't lying in wait for us somewhere.'

With his brother's assent the two ranchers headed east-north-east as best as Luke could orientate, heading, they hoped, for Austin.

The country they were in was unfamiliar to either of them. As they rode along in silence the landscape changed; the badlands gave way to a grass plain, although the vegetation was sparse in places. Then Luke saw something that made his heart stick in his throat.

A body.

As Luke moved closer he noticed something familiar about it. He jumped down off his horse, pushed the body on to its back with his boot, then let out a gasp. It was Bob Taggart, the ornery cuss of a ranch hand. Nate had ridden up beside his brother, now he looked down on the body.

'Damn! Is that Bob?'

'Yeah. The ranch hands were supposed be taking the herd – what's left of it, anyway – to Austin, to meet the trail drive. I was to meet up with them there. Seems ol' Bob didn't make it.'

'Look,' said Nate softly. 'There's more.'

In total they counted up four bodies, the remainder of the Driscoll hands.

'This is my fault, all my fault,' said Luke, holding his head in his hands.

'No, it's McTavish's fault – and we'll make sure the bastard pays for it.' Nate gritted his teeth. 'We've got to give these boys an honest burial. Not leave them for the vultures to scavenge.'

Luke shifted in his saddle. 'We better keep moving, Nate. I know these boys meant a lot to you, but if we don't keep . . . Nate!. *Nate!*'

Luke tried not to let the exasperation show on his face as his brother got off his mount and gingerly stepped around the dead bodies.

'No, Luke. We have to help them; bury them right.'

'It could be a trap. McTavish and his men could swoop down on us at any moment. And there's your leg—'

'I don't care a damn about my leg. I tell you, I'm going

to bury these boys. Now you can either help or get out of the way.'

There was iron in Nate's tone of voice and Luke could see the fury in his eyes. There was no point in arguing with him any further. Since they didn't have a shovel Luke persuaded his brother to build a cairn for the dead ranch hands. They collected the four bodies, Bob Taggart, Martin, Doug Eaton, and Charlie Navarro – the last of the Bar D hands – and laid them in a shallow dip.

It took Luke most of the day to scour the land for rocks big enough to build a basis for the cairn. Nate helped as much as he could but his leg wound hindered him from moving around. Luke made sure his brother got plenty of rest. Using his horse he dragged three big boulders to where they had laid the bodies. These served as the foundation stones. With his hands Luke dug a very shallow pit for each man and laid them inside, then with Nate's and his horse's help they pushed the boulders up to the men's graves. To make sure that no coyotes, vultures or other wildlife could reach the men Luke had placed a layer of pebbles over the bodies and used small rocks to fill in the gaps over each grave The boulders overlapped but didn't crush the bodies. A fitting resting place, he thought.

Perhaps, after this McTavish business was finished up, they would come back and have a proper ceremony for the men. In the meantime Luke found two sticks and with a ball of twine that he found on Charlie's body he created a makeshift cross. Satisfied with his handiwork he took a step back.

'Good job done, Luke. Now bow your head,' Nate said. Luke took off his hat and bowed his head as his brother mumbled a few words and a prayer.

'Thank you, Luke. Now we can go.'

Despite his exhaustion Luke was glad to hear Nate say that. The horses looked tired after pulling the boulders so Luke and Nate walked them slowly away from the place of death. Luke gave a shudder of relief when, eventually, the cairn was out of sight.

The sun was setting now and Luke wanted to make camp before it got dark. Before he could suggest this to Nate his brother mused:

'What do you think came of our herd, Luke?'

'I reckon McTavish's men took them, mixed them in with his herd and will most likely sell them at market.'

'I reckon you're right. Damn that man thrice over for what he's done!'

'We'll get him, Nate. Don't worry, justice will be ours.'

Nate nodded in reply and fell silent.

Luke worried that Nate might be becoming delirious with an infection in his leg wound. He called a halt for the night when they were barely four miles from the cairn. All through the night Luke watched his brother. Nate had the shakes and a fever that eventually broke. But Luke feared that worse was yet to come if he didn't get Nate some help in the next day.

In the morning Luke made a quick breakfast of rabbit meat and gave Nate more of the carefully rationed water. He needed to find a town soon or his brother would die from exposure. They rode on in silence; the horses having been rested Luke soon picked up the pace.

By the afternoon Luke's spirits were rising. He espied in the distance a rising column of smoke. Where there was smoke there was fire, either from a chimney or a camp-fire, and that meant people. He nudged Nate, who was drifting in and out of sleep, and pointed to the smoke.

'Let's see who it is,' he said. Nate nodded vigorously.

Cautiously they approached, Luke keeping one hand near his holstered gun. As they got closer to the column of smoke Luke could make out a small cluster of houses. The smoke was coming from an outlying building. A smokehouse perhaps? It was too small for living quarters. Luke figured it was situated in a collection of several farms, probably homesteaders who had come across in a wagon and decided to settle here. The settlement looked too big to be a single farm and too haphazard to call it a town. Still, close enough to civilization for their need. He only hoped they were friendly folk.

Luke trotted his horse up to the nearest long house, bypassing the smokehouse. Nate followed him slowly. Luke leaped off his mount and pounded on the door.

'Excuse me,' he called. 'We need help. I have a wounded man here. We're not outlaws, just honest cowboys,' he added, hoping to allay any fears the residents might have. Receiving no reply he tried again, speaking more loudly and desperately. At last he heard a high feminine voice.

'Go away,' it called. 'We have nothing of value here.'

Assuming it was a woman Luke tried again.

'Ma'am, please, my brother is wounded. We need someone to attend to him so he won't die. We mean you no harm, we swear it.'

The door opened and the business end of a Winchester poked out of the narrow opening.

'I said, go away. Or do I have to start shooting?'

106

Surprised, Luke backed up and raised his hands. He was about to speak when Nate suddenly fell off his horse. He turning toward him, his only concern being for his brother's health, so he didn't see the flash of a dress as the woman holding the rifle raced past him.

'You weren't lying. He really is hurt,' she said.

'Yes ma'am, hurt real bad, I think. I dressed him as best I could, but he needs water and rest – and maybe a doctor.'

'I'll get my husband. Wait here. Better give me your guns too, just in case.'

'In case what?'

'Someone shoots you.'

Reluctantly, Luke handed over his pistols and his rifle.

'Anything to save Nate,' he said.

'Wait here, don't go inside. I'll be back with more help.'

The woman, her blonde curls bobbing on her head, raced down the dirt path, leaving Luke to hold his passed-out brother all alone.

It wasn't long before she returned with half a dozen men, two mounted, the others on foot.

'See, they're here,' she said pointing. 'I took their guns. At least, from the one that was still standing.'

'Good job, Sally. We'll take it from here.'

One man stepped forward; his beard was wild and unkempt, his eyes darted back and forth.

'What are you fellas doing out here?'

'We got caught in an ambush,' Luke lied.

'Indians?'

'No ... um ... rustlers. We're all that's left of our drovers. Our herd is scattered to the four corners. My brother's shot, we need help.'

Luke thought it sounded plausible enough. He didn't want to scare these people into thinking there were Indian marauders about. It was easier to pass as cowboys, too, since that was a game of which both Luke and Nate knew the rules.

'Why don't you come inside then? My name's Ezekiel, you've already met Sally. I'll introduce you to the rest . . .' he waved his hand at the others gathered there, '. . . later. You can lay your friend—'

'Brother.'

'Brother, over there, on that bed.'

'He needs a doctor, he's lost a lot of blood.'

Ezekiel scoffed 'No doctor around here but we'll patch him up as best we can. Sally, bring me a bowl of water. Trust me friend. . . ?'

'Luke. Luke Driscoll.'

'Luke. I know what I'm doing.' The bearded farmer bent over Nate and examined his wound.

'You're lucky,' he said after a moment or two. 'I don't see any gangrene. Maybe we'll save his leg.'

Luke relaxed a little as the man worked on Nate while Sally kept moistening his mouth with a sponge soaked in water into his mouth. His brother would be OK, he hoped.

He stepped outside on to the porch to breathe in the fresh air. He noticed one of the men who had met them with Ezekiel ride off into the distance. He didn't think much of it at the time, but the forthcoming events would make him wish he had taken it seriously.

CHAPTER 15

Miranda rode at a hard gallop, not caring if she tired her horse. Speed was of the essence. With her mother's and sisters' help she had escaped from the McTavish ranch house. Disguised as a man, notionally one of the McTavish ranch's hands, she found her escape easy. Her sisters had helped with needle and thread to cut down a spare shirt and and pants belonging to her father while her mother had distracted her ever-present guard with new tasks to attend to.

Once he'd been distracted, cowed by her mother's overbearing demeanor, she slipped out of the house and on to the fastest horse her father owned that wasn't already in use. She hoped she wouldn't be too late. Her father had got word of where Luke and the elder Driscoll were and had left with most of his men to find them. He meant to finish them off and seize their land. She had seen the avarice in his eyes. Robert McTavish was no longer the man she had known as her father. He was something else entirely; it was as if a demon possessed him.

Her father had fifteen men with him. There was little

she could do against such odds, but she could get to Luke first to warn him, or at least be with him at the end. Miranda shuddered at that thought, and tried to keep her mind focused only on finding Luke.

Her father's men had had a head start, but they moved ponderously, stopping frequently: she could see that by the trail they had left. Not a skilled tracker, she had learned a little of the craft from one of her father's old friends when she was younger. David Baston was a good man, she had always been fond of him. No time for nostalgia now; he was long gone: a drifter, but he had taught her a few pointers that she put into practice now.

Eventually she slowed her horse, a great chestnut stallion, to conserve its strength. She had given it its head since she started, hoping to make up some ground, but now that she had picked up the trail she eased off a bit. Not sure of where they were going, Miranda could only speculate that Luke had tried to drive the remainder of his herd north. She hadn't come up with this supposition all on her own: actually she had overheard a couple of her father's men talking about it. Still, it made sense to her that Luke would try to make as much money for his brother as he could.

Coming over a rise Miranda suddenly stopped her horse. Below she could see her father, sitting astride his great black charger, directing his men. Even though she was perfectly disguised she was seized with a sense of alarm. Her mouth went dry and, though wanting nothing more than to escape, she froze in her saddle as she watched her father.

Then, shaking herself from her trance and realizing she could be spotted she dismounted and hid in a little copse near the trail. The men were milling about as her father barked orders. They seemed tired and inattentive.

Deciding she should eat Miranda unpacked the food her mother had provided. with her. She munched on trail jerky and then ate an apple. After a while, Miranda couldn't help drifting into sleep.

Before too long she woke up. Looking around she saw that her father and his crew were gone. Muttering a string of very unladylike words, she rushed to find her horse; it was grazing near by. She didn't know how long she had been asleep and, fearing she had lost valuable time, she remounted her horse and headed in the direction she thought her father would have gone. After a few minutes of hard riding Miranda realized that the trail had disappeared. She halted the horse. She realized that she lacked the tracking skills to pick up the trail again; she would have to go on her hunch.

She figured that her father would still be heading north, so she decided to continue in that direction until she could find some sign indicating that they had changed course. Already the terrain was becoming unfamiliar to her, and she knew that she risked getting lost. Regardless of possible danger and thinking of Luke, Miranda touched her spurs to her horse's sweaty flanks. The stallion reared once, then raced away, carrying Miranda northward.

To Luke, she hoped.

Luke sat on the porch absent-mindedly whittling a stick. Nate had woken up and was sitting in bed drinking a bowl of soup that Sally had brought him. The farmers hadn't talked much to them since their arrival, but they had been polite, giving them food and drink.

Ezekiel had worked silently on Nate's leg, cutting around the wound, washing it, getting all bone fragments out of it and finally dressing it. Ezekiel declared that all Nate needed was to rest for a while and that eventually his leg should be as good as new. Deeply appreciative of his ministrations though he was, Luke was anxious to leave, worried that Beaufort and his men would find them here.

He put down his knife and the whittled stick and walked inside, to find that his brother had finished the soup and was staring blankly out of the window. He blinked his eyes on seeing Luke.

'We've got to get out of here, Luke,' he said. 'These people, kind as they are, give me the hinkies. That old boy – Ezekiel – who worked on my leg wouldn't look me in the eye. There's something queer about him, and the way Sally keeps her distance, too.'

'Shh, keep your voice down, they might hear you,' warned Luke. 'They seem nice enough, but I agree – we've got to skedaddle as soon as you're ready. How are you feeling?'

'Better, still a little weak. Must have lost a lot of blood. But I'll be ready to go right after lunch. Pity to miss the opportunity of a decent meal.'

'Agreed. We'll eat, thank them for their hospitality and then go.'

Luke left to check their horses, which were stabled near by. It was almost noon so lunch wouldn't be far off. He would ask Sally to fix them up a pack of trail victuals, and then they'd be on their way. Wondering how he should thank Ezekiel, Sally and their fellow farmers Luke dug into his wallet. He found a few gold dollars, a three-dollar piece, a couple of stellas, and a double eagle.

He selected the double eagle: it would make a good repayment to Ezekiel for his kindness, he thought. Despite Nate's misgivings the farmer really had helped them. He didn't want to appear ungrateful to them but, at the same time, he didn't want to seem to insult them by offering them money. He decided to give the coin to Sally, discreetly. She could use it as she chose. That way his conscience would be clear.

Luke felt uneasy as he walked back to the main house. An eerie silence seemed to have descended on the small farming community. Luke couldn't see anyone, couldn't hear anyone either, which was unusual on a farm. Judging by what he had seen Luke thought they might be wheat farmers since they had fields, yet there were no threshers that he could see. There were no livestock noises either, no lowing of cows, or neighing of horses. Not even the wild birds were chirping. Luke suppressed a shudder and hurried quickly to the house. It was time to go; lunch be damned! They had to be out of this place.

When Luke opened the door his brother was sitting up, alert.

'Nate,' he said, 'we've got to go now.'

'Agreed, I think everyone's left. I called for Sally and Ezekiel and no one answered. Damn! I knew we shouldn't have trusted them.'

'We didn't know; anyway, in your condition you wouldn't have lasted long.'

'Don't worry about me, let's get before something bad happens.'

113

'Can you walk?'

Nate tested his leg gingerly. 'Yeah, I think I'll be OK. Did you saddle the horses?'

'They're ready to go.'

'Atta boy, Luke. Let's go – here, give me your arm.'

The two brothers strolled as casually as they dared out of the house. They got to their horses without anyone stopping them. Luke paused to check his ammunition, then said in a loud voice:

'Thank you for your hospitality. My brother is much better – on the mend, so we'll be leaving now. This is for your trouble.' He flung the double eagle down on the ground near the house and wheeled his horse, his brother following right behind him.

Then they saw, appearing from nowhere, Beaufort, Tobias, and their henchmen; their coats were flapping in the breeze, revealing their tied-down six shooters. Beaufort smiled, but before he could speak, Nate roared:

'Run them down. Come on, Luke.'

He charged the men at a full gallop. Luke, with only a moment's hesitation, followed him. A gunshot from behind revealed a shooter on the roof. Luke cursed: they were trapped. He followed his brother, though; it seemed the best strategy. Luke saw Beaufort's eyes open wide as Nate led the charge towards them. At the last moment he dived to the side while his men scrambled to safety.

Luke didn't look back, but he knew from the shouts and the subsequent gunshots that the men had drawn and fired.

Ahead lay open ground and safety. They rode on, Luke hardly aware that they were being pursued. Then he heard a shot and saw his brother pitch forward on his horse. Nate lay inert against the horse's neck. Luke grabbed his brother's reins, slowing his mount, and with superhuman effort he pulled him on to his own still moving horse. He kept riding. The shot had come from behind; he couldn't tell how close their pursuers were.

Luke's one thought was to put as much distance as possible between themselves and the gunmen and then to tend to his brother's fresh wound. It was no more than a wound, he felt sure. Nate would survive. Though their pursuers were out of sight for now he could hear them, and he feared the worst. Then, when he was sure his luck was running out he saw, to one side, a steep path rising to a small bluff. He guessed they were by now two or three miles from Ezekiel's farm. The bluff would put them on the higher ground, and maybe give them a chance to put even more distance between themselves and their pursuers.

Galloping at full speed he crested the summit. Looking behind Luke saw he had achieved more distance: Beaufort's men weren't directly behind them any more. They had been surprised by Nate's charge, and had scrambled to regroup for the chase; now the Driscoll brothers had left them in the dust.

Luke dismounted and laid Nate on the ground. He was still breathing, though shallowly, and his face was very pale. Luke worked quickly to try to get his brother's shirt off to attend to the wound but Nate put his hand on his wrist.

'Luke.' Nate's voice was a rasping gasp. 'Listen to me, I think I'm a goner.'

'No, Nate. We'll get you help. Just hold on.'

Nate slowly shook his head, the movement caused him pain.

'Shut up and listen,' he rasped. 'Take care of Maryanne for me, and get that bastard McTavish. I'm sorry about before, about our fight. I want to make my peace with you, Luke. I'm proud of you and I love . . .' his voice trailed off and soon his breathing stopped.

Luke shook him gently.

'Wake up, Nate. Nate, don't go.'

He wept softly to himself as his elder brother passed away.

More determined now than ever to make McTavish pay, Luke vowed revenge: a terrible vow that would have shocked most ordinary folk. Having no thought of leaving his brother's body, he secured it as firmly as he could to his own horse. Hoping he could make it to Austin before Beaufort and his henchmen caught up with him, he set off down the other side of the bluff, his heart hardened and deadly revenge in his eyes.

CHAPTER 16

Miranda was surprised when she saw the small community. At first she was glad to find civilization, a chance to eat, refresh and see a fellow human. But as she approached Miranda realized something was amiss. There were men on horseback all over the place, milling about, trying to get themslves organized. Heated words were being exchanged between the men on horseback and others on foot. Miranda was thanking her lucky stars for forewarning her when she heard her father's voice before he or anyone else had spotted her.

Frozen, she wanted to flee.

Then, when she had figured out that she really hadn't been seen, she slid off her horse and crept behind the nearest of the scattered houses. Close enough, she hoped, to hear without being caught.

'But Mr McTavish, we did as your men asked. When the Driscolls came to us we reported them right away. It was lucky that one of them was injured, otherwise they would have left right away. There's no call to be upset.'

'Damnation, Ezekiel! I wanted them caught once and for all, and now you're telling me they escaped?'

'Blame your hired gunmen. They had them and they let them go. We were told to stay out of the way, so we did.'

'I'll get to Beaufort soon enough. But I'm not paying you, not until they're caught.'

'But – but we need that money. All our crops have failed. If we don't have that money we'll starve. We've done as you asked.'

'Your crops are not my problem. Get me the Driscolls and I'll give you your money. Now, Ezekiel, in which direction did they go?'

'Toward Austin it looks like. Jeffro swears he clipped one of them.'

'Which one?'

'The elder brother.'

'Great. Let's get the men mounted up and we'll head them off. Oh, Ezekiel. Perhaps I was too hasty. My men need some supplies. Perhaps we could make an arrangement?'

The rest of what was said was muffled but Miranda had heard enough. Her Luke was still alive, but in trouble. Now she needed to get to him before her father did.

She leapt back on to her tired mount and rode briskly away from the farm.

It was a hard two days' ride to the outskirts of Austin. Luke's horse finally gave out a mile outside of town. The old gelding had been with him since his prospecting days, had served Luke faithfully. A single bullet to the head, his second from last, ended its suffering. Now Luke faced a dilemma: he had to carry his rapidly decomposing brother's body and his saddle the mile into Austin.

After adjusting his bandanna to cover his mouth and nose to help with the smell, he hefted Nate on to his shoulders and carried his saddle and trail pack. He only made it for a hundred feet before he collapsed.

As he sat there wondering what to do a wagon came by. The driver, a quizzical look on his face, slowly pulled on the reins.

'Need a hand? Is your friend hurt?'

'Dead. He's dead,' Luke croaked, his throat dry from disuse and lack of water.

'Oh, sorry to hear that. Need a lift to the undertaker's? I know right where one is.'

Luke nodded numbly. The wagon owner helped Luke place Nate's body gently on the flatbed. On the way into town Luke stayed mute, not wanting to explain what had happened. Wisely the driver didn't press him. The ride was short and, sooner than Luke wanted it to, the wagon stopped.

'Here you go, mister, one undertaker. Need help taking him inside?'

Luke nodded, still unable to recover his voice.

Once inside the wagoner doffed his hat, then hurried out as quickly as was decent. Luke couldn't blame him; it was not an occasion for social niceties. The undertaker came forward; he was a tall, thin, middle-aged man wearing a stovepipe hat.

'Ah. Another customer, I see. Oh, sorry; only a little undertaker humor. What happened?'

'Bullet in the back,' said Luke in as neutral a tone as he could muster.

'I see. Please come inside. Put the body there on that trestle table. My assistant will see to it. My name is

Gregory. This is Gregory's Funeral Parlor. Welcome. Please have a seat.'

Luke sat down in front of a big oaken desk. They were in a room adjacent to the entryway where Nate's body still lay on the trestle table. Gregory sat down behind the desk and took up pen and paper.

'Let's get started, shall we. Name of the deceased?'

'Nate, Nathan Driscoll.'

'And cause of death is bullet wound to the chest. I see no need to call the doctor; the man is surely dead. Um . . . relation to the deceased?'

'Brother.'

'Ah, my sincere condolences. Where will he be buried?'

'Here – in Austin,' Luke replied blankly.

'Yes, but which cemetery?'

'I'm not sure, I'll have to ask his wife.' *Oh no, Maryanne!* He had to find her and tell her. 'How much will this be?'

'Humm, let's see. We have to dress the body, then there's the coffin and the burial plot. Depending on the cemetery, you might be looking at fifty to sixty dollars, at the minimum.'

Luke swallowed hard, realized his throat was still dry and asked for a drink of water. Fifty dollars was more money than he had on him. Damnation! He wished he hadn't given away that double eagle to those treacherous farmers.

When the undertaker returned with the water, Luke's mind was spinning. After taking a drink he dropped a five-dollar piece on Mr Gregory's desk.

'Here,' he said. 'This should suffice as a down

payment, until I talk to the widow.'

Gregory frowned.

'This is highly unusual. . . .' He hesitated and took one look at Luke's face; he saw the grim determination in the man's eyes and finished with '. . . but considering the circumstances I will gladly accept the down payment.'

'Greatly appreciated, Mr Gregory. I'll be back as soon as I can. Take care of my brother.'

'Yes, yes. Rest assured – he is in the best of hands.'

The two men shook and Luke departed. Now all he had to do was find and tell Maryanne that her husband was dead. Where to look in a city the size of Austin? He wandered down the street, anxiously wondering what to do when he saw a big bold sign hanging over a tall building to his left: Austin Gazette. A newspaper. Luke had an idea. He entered through the main door and walked up to a small enquiry desk.

'How much to place a classified advertisement in the paper?' he asked the clerk.

'That depends on the word count.' The clerk pushed his glasses up his nose. 'The charge is two bits per word.'

'Could I borrow a pen and paper please?' Luke hastily wrote down what he wished to say: *For Maryanne Driscoll, Please find Luke at . . .* He looked up at the clerk.

'What's the nearest saloon?'

'The Broken Wagon is just a block down the street from here.'

'Does it let rooms?'

'Oh yes. Not very classy but respectable enough.'

'It will do. Thanks.' He finished the message by adding that Maryanne should find him at the Broken Wagon saloon.

'You print an evening edition? Great, make sure this gets out in it.' He paid the man and got directions to the saloon. He hoped Maryanne would read the newspaper.

Now he could only wait.

At last Miranda had arrived in Austin. She had had the good fortune to be picked up by a traveling family. They were in a covered wagon, which made for slower but safer travel. Although perhaps not entirely convinced by Miranda's assurances that she had firm arrangements to meet a friend in the city they had nevertheless left her, as she requested, in the main square before trundling away to their own destination.

That she had managed to avoid being spotted by her father's men at the farmers' settlement had at first filled her with a sense of confidence. Now, alone amidst the bustle of an unfamiliar city going about its business, she realized that she had no idea where to find Luke, or even if he was still in the city. Her false confidence had given way to a sense of unease. She led her horse towards a water trough, aware that if she remained so obviously uncertain where to go in this public place she could attract unwanted attention.

The most obvious places to look for a single man in a big city were, of course: the saloons. But there could be no question of her, a young, respectable woman, entering saloons unaccompanied in search of a single man. Glancing about her, she saw that there were two or three saloons within view. Outside each one several horses were tethered. A thought suddenly struck her. She could not search inside the saloons for Luke, but perhaps she could look *outside* them for his horse, which she would have no difficulty in recognizing. She could not know, of course, that Luke had had to shoot his horse out on the highway after the death of Nate.

She crossed the square to one of the saloons; none of the three horses outside was Luke's. Neither was any of the six mounts that stood tethered outside the next saloon. She was just recrossing the square to go to the third saloon when she heard her name called by a familiar voice. *Luke!* her wishful heart told her. *He's found me.* But even before she had twisted in her saddle to look at the man who had uttered her name she realized that, though the voice was familiar, it wasn't Luke's. Checking herself, for she did not wish to meet his gaze, she froze as his horse's flank brushed against her knee.

'Miss Miranda,' the voice said again.

Zach! How could I ever have mistaken his voice for Luke's?

'Your father is worried sick about you, Miss Miranda. One of our scouts saw you ride away from the farm. It is fortunate that I've found you here. A big city can be a dangerous place for a woman.' He put out a hand to take hold of her mount's bridle.

'Are you taking me to him, Zack?'

'Yes, Miss Miranda, those are my orders.'

'But if he doesn't know I'm here, he need never know you found me. You can let me go and Daddy will never know the difference.'

Zack shook his head. 'Afraid I can't do that, Miss Miranda. I've got to tell your father.'

Miranda knew that she was defeated; she lowered her head. She had come so close to Luke, only to be corralled now, like a maverick cow, by her father's man.

To her mortification Zack produced a length of rope and attached it to her horse's bridle to serve as a leading rein. He took her down the street until they came to a hotel with an impressive frontage. Gleaming brass letters across the pediment of the pillared entrance spelled out its name: THE IMPERIAL. Well, that figured, Miranda thought; her father would always stay in the grandest place in town.

Zack dismounted and nodded to Miranda, indicating that she should do the same. Then he tethered both horses to the hitch rail. Taking Miranda firmly by one elbow he guided her up the steps and in to the hotel's elegantly furnished foyer. Pausing only briefly to nod to the desk clerk he guided Miranda up a broad flight of thickly carpeted stairs and along a corridor. He knocked on the third door on the right.

'Come.'

A flutter of chilly apprehension took wing in Miranda's stomach as she recognized her father's voice. And there, as Zach opened the door, she saw him, sitting expectantly behind a large oaken desk.

'Thank you, Zachary. You've done a good job – at last,' he said.

'Will there be anything else, Mr McTavish?'

'No, you may leave me, but wait downstairs in the foyer.'

As the door closed behind Zach Miranda swallowed hard. There was a long silence while McTavish studied his daughter, as though his eyes were peering into her very soul. Miranda resisted the urge to run screaming from the room.

At last, his hands steepled together, Robert McTavish

leaned forward.

'Hello, my dear. So good to see you here in Austin. Please have a seat. Let us discuss family loyalty.'

CHAPTER 17

It didn't take long for Maryanne to find Luke. By good fortune her sister read the paper regularly and she told Maryanne about the message in the classifieds.

He had been sitting by the bar when, her eyes filled with worry, she walked in. Gently Luke led her by the hand to the privacy of his room.

'Maryanne, I think it would be better if you sat down. There's something I need to tell you about Nate.'

'He's dead isn't he? I can see it written on your face,' she said in a barely audible whisper. Luke found he couldn't respond in words, all he could manage was a nod. He thought he had mentally prepared himself to deal with the grief of his brother's widow, but now she started crying and he could feel his own control weakening. Then suddenly she stopped. Wiping a tear from her eye she said:

'Was it that bastard McTavish?'

'One of his men, yeah.'

'Kill 'em, Luke. Kill 'em all. Avenge your brother,' she replied with venom.

'Don't worry, Maryanne, he'll get his just deserts.'

She nodded, 'Where's the body? Did you leave it some-where for McTavish to truss up?'

'No indeed; I brought it here. He's at the undertaker's – Gregory's Funeral Parlor, over on Baker Street. There's a ... um ... small question of price for the burial.'

'Don't worry. I'll take care of it. I'll give my man a proper funeral.'

'Let me know when you want to bury him. I'll be there.'

'Will you find McTavish?' she asked, hope filling her voice.

'I'll find him, but first I need to talk to the marshal. I want to make sure I'm on the right side of the law when I go gunning for the wretch.'

Maryanne nodded. 'That's fine, Luke. When you finish your business with McTavish we'll have the funeral. Could I ask you to see yourself out, please, and leave a widow to her grief?'

Luke, somewhat relieved to have got this difficult task over and done with, left her sobbing quietly as he shut the door.

Then he went to find the marshal.

'And you have proof that Mr Robert McTavish murdered your brother?' asked the marshal, who had introduced himself as Ted Bartlett. He raised a sceptical eyebrow.

'You have to believe me. He's after my brother's land. His widow might be in danger too.'

'Mr ... Driscoll is it? You come in here weaving tall tales and expect me to believe you without any evidence?' Marshal Bartlett shook his head, 'That ain't how it works. You've got to have proof, and a warrant signed by a judge.

Why haven't you gone to Sheriff Collins in Garrison?'

'He don't seem able to see the evidence in front of his eyes,' Luke told him. He wondered if he was right in sensing that Bartlett seemed unsurprised.

'Hm. Well now, if you ask me nicely maybe I can ask one of my deputies to look into it. But I'm warning you, Driscoll, if you're lying we'll bring charges against you. Samuel, *Samuel!*' Bartlett yelled out.

'Yes sir?' A short skinny youth who didn't look old enough to shave popped his head through the door.

'Deputy Wilkins here will assist you with this investigation. Sam, go with Mr Driscoll and see what you can dig up on a Robert McTavish over in Sutton County. Now are you satisfied, Mr Driscoll? Good. Let me get back to more important matters.'

'He sure was helpful.' Luke groused outside the office.

'Don't mind Ted. He's always like that. Now, are we riding to Sutton county?' asked Sam.

'Yeah, but I have to settle my bill first and talk to my brother's widow.'

When they arrived back at the Broken Wagon saloon Luke walked up to the bartender.

'I need to pay my bill, last name Driscoll.'

The swarthy-complexioned man looked up from polishing a glass and took a quick glance at his account books.

'Luke Driscoll? That'll be four dollars for the room. Oh yeah, this note was left for you too.'

Luke paid the man and took the note. His blood ran cold as he read what it said.

Come alone outside the city near mile marker ten if you want

128

to see Miranda alive again.

He handed the note over to the deputy.

'If this isn't proof that McTavish is a dirty skunk I don't know what is.'

'What does it mean?' asked Sam when he too had read it.

'It means he's keeping his daughter Miranda as hostage until I come to him. Come on, he wants to meet me out of town.'

'Maybe you should wait until I report this to the boss.'

'That's fair. I'll wait – but not for long,' growled Luke.

Sam nodded and left with the note, presumably to tell the sceptical Marshal Bartlett. Hoping that he would at last get the backing of the law Luke went outside to the boardwalk. Feeling frustrated, it seemed that all he could do was just sit around and wait for the law to get organized. He decided to wait for Sam outside the city and stepped down from the boardwalk. He hadn't gone more than ten yards when, out of the shadow of a building, stepped Reginald Beaufort. Luke turned around and saw his henchman, Tobias, standing behind him.

'Now, now, Mr Driscoll, there's no call to be nervous. We're here only as your escort. To make sure you get to where you need to be without interference from the authorities. Do you have the note we left you?'

Luke shook his head in disgust.

'I had it, but I threw it away.'

'So be it. Tobias, would you lead the way? I shall accompany Mr Driscoll.'

Luke saw other men step out of the shadows. There seemed no way out of this.

He was trapped.

Luke glanced sideways as he walked slowly to the outskirts of town. There were ten men now surrounding him, all carrying Colts on their holsters. He was outnumbered and outgunned: McTavish wasn't taking any chances. He darted his gaze to and fro, trying to find a way to escape. Beaufort looked at him with a sneer, Tobias favored him with a condescending smile. Trapped, Luke sighed. The hired gunslingers had got him.

'Real shame about your brother. Our employer was looking forward to seeing him swing. Too bad, guess he'll have to be satisfied with you. The last obstacle.'

'Not quite the last, Beaufort.' Tobias spoke up.

'True, Tobias, too true; there is the dear widow Driscoll to think of. Perhaps we'll be tasked to bring her in, after spending a little time with her first, of course.' Beaufort rubbed his hands with glee. Luke reached for the man's shirt but instantly four pairs of hands held him back.

'Meet me man-to-man, Beaufort. Call off your dogs, and we'll see how brave you really are. If you touch Maryanne I'll break every thrice-damned bone in your body.'

Beaufort gave an amused smile, then slowly shook his head.

'The time for parleying is over, Driscoll,' he said. 'You're about to meet the hangman. You can leave that young widow – Maryanne, is it? – to us.'

Luke tried to lunge at Beaufort but now six men held him back, forcing him to the ground, belaboring him with their fists.

130

Luke did his best to cover his head as blows rained down on him. Eventually Beaufort called on them to stop and the men hauled Luke to his feet, bloody and battered.

'I think McTavish is going to enjoy breaking your spirit. If not him, then I sure will. Now, threaten me again and I'll have your arms broken. McTavish said to bring you in alive, but he didn't say unscathed.'

Luke's eyes burned into Beaufort's but he held his tongue. It would do no good to lose his temper only to bring more violence upon himself. He needed to even the odds – and soon: they were almost out of town. As they walked Luke deliberately slowed his pace, hoping that he could stall long enough for Deputy Wilkins to show up. This tactic soon failed.

'Drag him if he walks any slower,' Beaufort said. 'We've got an appointment to keep.'

Soon they were out of Austin, away from any possible help. He was marched away from the road, further and further into the wilderness that surrounded the town.

The group stopped in front of a lone elm tree; a rope dangled from one of its branches.. Luke's hands were tied tightly behind him. His heart nearly stopped when he saw, coming out of the shadows behind the elm, a group riding toward them.

It was McTavish, and Miranda was with him.

Miranda looked on aghast as Luke was brought forward. Her father, ignoring her distress, leered at him. Relishing his moment, the rancher leaned back in the saddle. He turned to one of the group of men.

'The brother is dead?'

131

The man nodded. 'Yup, Tobias confirmed it a little while ago with the mortician.'

'So, then this is the last one, eh?'

'There's the widow too, she's making burial arrangements right now.'

'Huh! She's no threat. Without her husband or brother-in-law she'll fold. All right, boys. Let's string him up and go back home. Beaufort, you and I have to settle accounts.'

At last Miranda, her heart frozen with fear at her father's words, found her voice.

'Father, you can't. Please. . . .'

'No, Miranda, you'll have no more to do with Driscoll. He is a criminal, trespassing on land that is *rightfully* mine, and now he's going to get his *rightful* punishment.' He turned to the man he had been speaking to. 'Get him on a horse, and hold back my daughter.'

As the men were attempting to get the struggling Luke on to a skittish mare Miranda saw a cloud of dust. It was moving rapidly toward them and picking up speed.

'Look!' she cried, pointing. What's that!'

'Could be a posse. The marshal's deputy has seen your note about our little meeting here,' said Luke, a wry smile on his face.

'What note?' McTavish asked.

Tobias doffed his hat. 'We left a note for Luke at the bar, so's he could find us easily.' He spoke with a little leer at his own joke, but the expression was smartly wiped off his face.

'You left a what . . . a *note*? And now the law has it?' McTavish roared with incredulity. Tobias and Luke both nodded.

'Hell's bells! That must be the dumbest thing I've ever heard of. Someone climb that tree and see whether it really is the law.'

A man hurriedly scrambled up the elm tree.

'Yup, it's the law dogs,' he shouted down. 'I see the sun glinting off the badges of some of 'em.'

'Tarnation! Cut that rope and let's skedaddle.' McTavish gave Luke a hard look.

'Let this be a warning to you, Driscoll,' he said. 'Stay away from my land and my daughter. You take your brother's widow and you get as far away from Texas as you can. Because if you don't – if I catch wind of you snooping around my land – I'll string you up. This rope here,' he held up the noose, 'has got your name on it. Your brother's land is mine now. Let's move boys.'

McTavish turned his horse and dug his spurs deep into its flanks. Two men, one pulling the reins of Miranda's horse, the other riding close behind, forced her to follow him. Miranda dared a glance over her shoulder and saw her beloved sitting ahorse, his hands still tied, but alive.

Her heart ached as they parted once again, but she hoped he would heed her father's words and be safe.

CHAPTER 18

Luke watched McTavish turn tail and flee. For a moment he was alone, he let out his breath in big gasps, not realizing how hard his heart had been pounding. He had come close to death only a moment before. Finally the posse rode up, a group of ten men, led by Deputy Sam Wilkins.

'Am I glad you showed up,' Luke drawled when Sam came over to him.

'Better late than never. Can I give you a hand?' Luke shrugged as Sam cut his bonds. Rubbing his hands to restore the circulation he looked at Sam with appreciation. His hand shook ever so slightly as he extended it.

'Much obliged for the help, Sam.'

'Any time, friend. Where did McTavish go? He was here – right?'

'He was here but he hightailed it when he saw you coming. We can still catch him if we hurry.'

Sam frowned. 'Marshal Bartlett'll need a warrant first, and justifiable cause for that. What exactly did he do again?'

'He killed my brother, kidnapped his daughter and

almost had me strung up.'

'And you have evidence of all that?'

'My brother's body, he's got a bullet in him.'

'Put there by McTavish?'

Luke paused, 'No not McTavish, but one of his men. Maybe, I didn't see who actually shot him.'

Sam sighed, 'Yeah, sure. Let's go into town and talk about it with the marshal. Ted's a stickler for the rules and on a few areas we can find flexibility but on this I think he'll abide by the book. With a man of McTavish's stature we're going to have to get a lot of evidence to bring him in.'

Luke opened his mouth to argue but then thought better of it. If he couldn't get the marshal on his side, so help him: he'd go the the state governor.

Back at the station Marshal Bartlett took as dim a view of Luke's story as Sam did.

'So this farm where you say your brother was shot was run by a man named Ezekiel. Not Ezekiel Jessup was it?'

'I didn't get their last names,' replied Luke.

'Probably one and the same, sounds like him anyway. Sam, you got that Wanted poster for Jessup? Thanks. Now, this man Ezekiel is wanted for fraud up in Missouri. He came down here masquerading as a cult leader a few months back. Jessup went off into the wilds to live off the land as he put it with a few people he called his followers, more likely his partners in crime, and we haven't seen him since. It's possible one of them might have shot your brother, and I'm betting that's what McTavish, or McTavish's lawyers, will say.'

Luke tried to protest. 'But what about Miranda? She was held against her will, I know it.'

'Did she say as much?'

'No, she didn't but . . .'

Bartlett waved his hand. 'Now we can go on and on like this but, son, I need hard evidence. If I don't have it . . . but I'll tell you what I'll do. If Sam here is willing, he can take a few volunteers in an unofficial investigative capacity to find your evidence. He likes you well enough. I don't but he does. And if you find evidence then we can get a warrant and arrest Robert McTavish. Is that fair? But no shooting though. I don't want any of my men shot up by some trigger happy cowboy who wants to settle scores.'

Luke lowered his eyes, hesitated and then reluctantly he said 'If it's the best I can do?'

'It is.'

'Then I accept.'

'Great, Sam can arrange the details. Now get out of my office, I've got real work to do. Oh, thanks for the tip on Ezekiel, I might send a welcoming party up his way, see if we can bring him in.' With that Marshal Bartlett leaned back in his chair and lowered his hat to shade his eyes. Luke snorted in disgust and left.

Once outside in the fading sunlight Luke turned to Sam.

'Thanks, I appreciate the help. We've got to go to the McTavish spread to uncover any evidence.'

'I reckon that is true.'

'I've got to see how my brother's funeral preparations are going. Can we meet back here in a couple of hours?'

'We'll leave in the morning. I've got too much to do right now. I'll see how many others I can find to come too.'

Luke thanked the deputy again and headed to the

mortuary. There he met Maryanne.

'Did you find McTavish?' she asked eagerly when he entered.

Luke grimaced 'He's back at his ranch. I thought I'd see to Nate's funeral first.'

'We're about ready to bury him. I bought a plot outside of town and I located a priest to give the service.'

'Great, when's the funeral.'

'As soon as my sister gets here; ah, there she is now.'

Luke looked up as in walked a middle-aged blonde woman accompanied by a tall thin man with graying hair at the temples.

'Luke, please meet my sister Beth Henshaw and her husband Jim; he's a butcher.'

After pleasantries were exchanged the four of them left the mortuary in two carriages following a buckboard carrying Nathan Driscoll's body. When the funeral had finished, the priest was gone, and Jim and Beth Henshaw had departed, Luke and Maryanne stood alone by the grave of the man they each loved most in the world.

'Tell me, Luke, tell me what came between you and Nate? I know there was something, tell me please.'

Luke waited a long moment before answering her, his mind filled with memories of him and his brother. She was earnest in her pleadings, she deserved to know.

'I'll tell you,' he said, 'though it shouldn't concern you now.'

Maryanne urged him to continue.

'There was a woman. A fiery woman named Cassandra whom Nate loved, and I stole her from him. But I couldn't keep her. Her heart was wild, one I couldn't tame. She went off with another man, so I got what I deserved, I guess. But Nate was stubborn and wouldn't let it go. This was after Ma and Pa died, so I pulled up stakes and left, ending up in Montana. Then I got his letter, so I came back. But look, Maryanne, he loved you most of all.'

Luke looked at her nervously. Her eyes glittered, unreadable. At last she gave a faint smile.

'I know he loved me. I appreciate you telling me, Luke. Now find that bastard McTavish and kill him. He took my Nate from me, he deserves the same fate. For the life of your brother's unborn child do it. If you don't I swear I'll do it myself.' There was something terrible in her voice, trembling, full of fury. Luke was taken aback, his face was pale.

Eventually he rallied and said 'I'll see that justice comes to him.'

She seemed satisfied by his answer.

'Thank you, Luke. Thank you, let me know when it's done. I'll be at my sister's. Oh, here's the address so you don't have to use the newspaper again.'

With that she turned from the graveside and walked away without looking back. Left alone Luke at last broke down and, in his grief, pent up for days, he wept until darkness lay across the land.

The next day Luke left Austin with Deputy Wilkins and three other, temporary, deputies and headed for the Bar D ranch. He only hoped he could find evidence in the burned-out ranch house or elsewhere that would implicate McTavish.

Luke flicked the reins of his newly acquired horse. It was so good of McTavish to have left him the horse he'd intended Luke to swing from. With a fresh mount, plenty of ammunition, and a fully stocked travel pack Luke was ready to meet the man who had intended to destroy Nate and all that Nate had worked for. Sam was talkative along the way. His fellow deputies were less loquacious; in fact they spoke hardly at all, preferring monosyllabic comments or replies.

Sam only introduced them by their first names: Frank, a tall, older, serious-looking man, and the two younger deputies Josh and Logan. They only nodded briefly. Sam said the deputies preferred to focus on their task, and Luke didn't pry into their thoughts on the matter in hand.. So the five of them rode on with the chatter of cheerful Sam helping to eat up the road.

A few hours out of Austin the riders saw another, larger, group heading toward them. Nervous, Luke started to reach for his piece, but Sam held up his hand. He rode forward and greeted the the group. Luke watched as an animated conversation took place, then frowned as Sam and the lead rider came toward him. Sam was smiling.

'This here is Luke Driscoll. Luke, meet Adam Parker, he's a deputy from Sheriff Collins' office in Garrison. Seems the sheriff is indisposed, so Adam has agreed to lead some men from Garrison to help us.'

'You have my thanks, Deputy Parker. I hope we won't need them, but McTavish has a large outfit, and he's unpredictable,' said Luke.

The newly enlarged group continued on to Garrison. The five new lawmen fell in with their brethren, and Sam picked up his earlier lively talk; his dream was to break a big case, or bring in a named gunslinger, so far both had eluded him. Luke asked him if he had heard

139

of a gunslinger named Beaufort, but Sam, after pondering a moment, said he had never heard of him. Not infamous enough apparently, thought Luke, but then Beaufort and his men reckoned to operate on the windy side of the law. Perhaps that's how they kept their names off the Wanted posters.

They made good time: so much so that Sam declared they could make it to Garrison by the following day. Luke felt relief, even more so when Sam and the other deputies decided to camp outdoors. Better to avoid other people at this juncture in case McTavish got word of their arrival. The lawmen congregated together leaving Luke alone. Better this way Luke thought, keeping a distance between him and the law.

He dreamed of Miranda that night. The next morning dawned bright and Luke and the lawmen got an early start. He wanted to bring them first to the Bar D so that the lawmen could assess the damage and then confront McTavish.

By the time the party arrived it was late afternoon. The remains of the burned-out ranch house, his brother's life's labor, still stood: a few charred stanchions standing bleakly among the ashes. Luke eyed Deputy Parker and said:

'This is the place. My brother's ranch house, burned to the ground by McTavish's hoods.' Luke looked hopeful as the lawmen got down in the rubble, searching for clues. After a while Sam came back to Luke.

'There's not much here to tell us what happened. Could have been a lightning strike, or a carelessly unattended lamp, or anything. How do we know McTavish did this?'

'Because he was the only one who could have done so,'

Luke set his jaw, and started to grind his teeth.

'Any witnesses?'

'None living. No, wait. McTavish's daughter was here. He might have told her what happened, she could give you evidence if she was willing to talk.'

Sam scratched his chin, 'We can go and talk to her, but if she doesn't want to implicate her father there's nothing we can do to compel her to testify.'

'I understand.' Luke figured she wouldn't want to talk in front of her father or his men, but if he could get her alone then there might be a chance she'd tell the truth about Robert McTavish.

'I can see if she'll talk to me alone. Maybe then she'll feel free to talk about her father.'

Sam narrowed his eyes. 'No way. You're going to stay far away from McTavish's daughter until we get this mess figured out. Wait here; we'll go to the McTavish ranch ourselves.'

Luke grudgingly agreed to Sam's logic, although he suspected McTavish wouldn't let anyone see his daughter. The lawmen took their departure, leaving Luke to build a campfire as dusk set in.

By the time Sam and his men returned it was well past dark. Luke rose to his feet as they approached.

'We had no luck trying to speaking with Miranda; her mother told us she was indisposed. But Robert McTavish talked to us. He said that you and your brother are squatters on his land, and that's the cause of the dispute between you. He denied torching your brother's ranch house.' Sam stood with folded arms, looking at him expectantly.

'That's utter bollocks. Nate had this land long before McTavish showed up. Check the county records to get the truth.'

'That has already been done.'

As Luke looked at Sam's face he remembered what Nate had told him when he first arrived: *the sheriff's in his pocket.* Now he understood what his brother had meant. McTavish had been cooking the books, changing the records, getting the law on his side. Now he was keeping Miranda from speaking out for him.

Luke wanted to let out a howl of frustration. Instead he simply bowed his head and stood there silently, defeated.

CHAPTER 19

In the morning, as Wilkins and his men prepared to return to Austin, Luke saddled up and followed Sam out of the campsite.

'We'll go and talk to Sheriff Collins in Garrison, then go back to Austin. For what it's worth, I'm sorry. I think McTavish has probably done you wrong, but there's no way we can arrest him without compelling proof.'

'I know,' Luke muttered. They continued on their way in silence for a short while, Luke's thoughts in a stew all the time. They came across a small number of cattle being herded by two of McTavish's men, who leered and hooted as they went by. Luke tried to ignore them; then, staring at the beefers, he saw one with the Bar D brand on it. A stray, perhaps, that had been picked up by the other rancher? Then he saw another – and another. The whole herd, thirty cows in all, were Bar D property. His heart skipped a beat; this was surely evidence enough for the lawmen. He halted his steed and edged in for a closer look. Realizing his intention, one of the cowboys saw him and moved to stop him. The commotion caused the lawmen to turn around.

'What's going on?'

'Sam, here is your proof that McTavish is dirty, These beefers belong to my brother, see the Bar D brand? McTavish is so arrogant he forgot to rebrand them.'

Luke leapt off his horse and examined the nearest cow more closely. His initial assumption was incorrect: McTavish had tried to rebrand the cattle – Luke could see the big M over a curved line – but it was off kilter, not square on the Bar D; it looked as though it had been hastily done. Not all of the cattle had been rebranded. He saw one at least with only the Driscoll brand. A rough hand grabbed him from behind.

'When the boss hears about this he's gonna ride you out of town on a rail.' It was one of the drovers. He was big, his arms corded with muscle, and his grip was like a vice. He spun Luke around to face him, his right hand was curled into a meaty fist.

'Stop!' Sam had got off his horse and was bulling his way between the two combatants. 'What's going on?'

Luke quickly explained the brands used by his brother and McTavish, and how it was now clear that McTavish had stolen from his brother's herd.

'This does warrant further investigation.' The lawman turned to the burly drover. 'Where's your boss? We need to talk to him.'

'He's busy.'

'Indeed. I imagine he won't be too busy for us. Take us to him now.'

The drover hesitated; he still hadn't let go of Luke's shirt but he lowered his fist.

'Fine. I'll take you.' The big man looked at his partner, who had remained mounted. 'Go get the boss. Tell him the law wants to see him.'

'Fair enough. You'll wait here until he comes,' said Sam. The big man nodded and slowly released his grip on Luke.

They didn't have to wait long for McTavish to show up with ten more men. Luke had a nervous feeling about this. He stood beside Sam as McTavish dismounted.

'I hear there is a problem with my cattle?' No words of greeting; he came briskly to the point. Sam nodded.

'Yes. Would you care to explain the differences in the brands on your cows?'

McTavish looked over the beefers that Sam was pointing to.

'That's easy,' he replied. 'Driscoll's brother stole cows from my herd. That's why we're having the dispute in the first place. You brought me all the way out here for this?'

Sam squinted at the brands.

'Your brand looks fresh on this cow, while the Bar D seems old. Also there seem to be some cows with no brand at all. I suspect you've been rustling cattle.'

McTavish gave a manic grin.

'Eh, if that's the way you want to play it . . .' he said in a low, menacing tone.

As though on a sudden inspiration Luke reached for his gun and fired a shot into the air before McTavish could finish speaking. The lawmen and McTavish's crew froze where they stood. Then all hell broke loose. Luke's shot, as he had intended, had spooked the cattle.

They started stampeding, screening Luke and the lawmen from McTavish.

'Don't shoot the cows,' roared McTavish. The stampede gave the lawmen enough time to get back to their horses. Luke took another shot, this time his aim was true, one of the punchers collapsed. He quickly followed Sam. McTavish's men recovered from the confusion and seeing the fleeing lawmen tried to run them down. The four now-mounted lawmen turned and shot in quick succession, felling three more men. Luke looked in awe at the precision of the lawmen but didn't have time to stop and wonder. He made it to his horse and met up with the lawmen. McTavish's drovers were milling about in confusion, hesitant to charge the deadly quartet and Luke.

'Come on,' shouted McTavish, 'Back to the ranch, we'll get the others. We can't let those lawmen leave alive.' Loyal to the brand and their cruel boss the remaining hands followed. Luke held his breath, only now realizing that his heart was beating fast.

'Looks like you've got your evidence,' Sam said quietly. 'What'll we do now?'

'Arrest McTavish for cattle rustling and attempted murder of lawmen.'

Luke grinned. 'Sounds good to me. But he's got lots of men with him, and now that he's already taken shots at you, he's sure to try and finish the job. No way he wants to let us live.'

'Right, so any ideas as to how to beat him? You know his lands as well as anybody.'

Luke thought for a moment.

'Yeah,' he said, 'I have an idea. I know the perfect place for an ambush. We can wait there for him to come to us. Take out enough of his men and then we'll have him.'

'Sounds excellent, I'll get the men in position.'

*

The ambush site was the same place Luke had used to buy time for his drovers to collect the herd. It would serve their purposes, he thought, since it had a clear line to the McTavish ranch. By the time the ten of them arrived McTavish was assembling a large force of his men in front of the large ranch house. Luke and Sam took point while the other three Rangers hung back, hidden among the trees.

'With one clear shot, I can take him out,' said Luke, eagerly fingering his Winchester.

Sam raised one finger. 'Nope, we do this the legal way. I won't condone murder.' Then he raised his voice. 'Robert McTavish, you are under arrest for cattle rustling and the attempted murder of law officers. Please raise your hands and turn yourself in peacefully!'

Luke saw McTavish raise one hand. Almost at once a score or more of his men began to charge, some on horseback and others afoot.

'So that's how he wants it,' Sam muttered. 'Get ready, boys.'

Shots started to rain down amongst them, one barely missing Luke's shoulder.

'Fall back,' yelled Sam, 'they're coming up too fast.'

Luke obliged Sam but not before he'd got off two quick shots, neither of which hit anything.

The lawmen behind them laid down covering fire, opening up with their rifles as Luke and Sam moved further up the slope. McTavish's men, with bloodlust in their eyes, kept coming. An undisciplined mob, they would depend upon their sheer numbers to overwhelm the lawmen.

'Come on – closer to the summit. We can make a stand there.' Luke urged them. Once they'd reached the summit, the pursuit slowed.

Now the law officers had the high ground with the further advantage that the slope was steepest near the top. Sam's men were in their element; backs to the wall, they bore down and rained death on McTavish's men. Luke kept up with the furious pace, pumping his Winchester faster than he ever had done before. Through the gunsmoke he could see that he'd felled three or maybe five of McTavish's men. The onslaught proved to be too much for the rannies. By ones and twos they broke and ran back down the hill, leaving the wounded where they lay.

Luke took some deep breaths.

'That was a close one. I'm sure glad you guys are here.'

'I haven't been involved in a firefight like that before. Frank, your guys all right?' Sam asked one of his deputies. Frank confirmed that no one had been wounded.

'We got lucky,' said Sam. 'Now for the hard part – getting to McTavish himself.'

'Do you think we've thinned them out enough, taken the fight out of his ranch hands?' asked Luke.

'We'll find out in a minute. Nothing for it now but to press our advantage. Let's head down to the house. Look out for his family, boys – we got no quarrel with them.'

The lawmen moved quickly down the hill, ignoring the cries of the wounded ranch hands. One man tried to pull his gun but Luke swatted him down with his rifle butt.

As they were coming down the hill at full charge Luke let loose a bloodcurdling Rebel yell. The few cowboys who were still able to move turned at the sound, to see five angry fully armed men charging them. Demoralized, they put up little resistance. Most fled, others dropped their weapons and raised their hands. Only two men tried to take aim, but they were quickly gunned down. The lawmen stormed the house. Some minutes later they came out again.

Luke grabbed one of the men by the arm and shook him.

'McTavish, where is he?' he shouted, his eyes ablaze. The man stuttered, unable for the moment to speak. Then, as Luke grabbed his shoulders and shook him, he blurted out:

'He's gone. He's fled with his family to the Outpost.'

Luke gave him a searching look.

'What's the Outpost?'

The man looked down to the ground, avoiding eye contact. Luke shook him again.

Still with his eyes cast down the man replied:

'It's his secret hideout on the far side of the range, due north.'

Luke let the man go and he collapsed on the ground. Sam was now approaching.

'I know where McTavish is,' Luke told him.

'Great. Let's go. We'll leave Frank and the others to keep tabs on these men – and in case McTavish doubles back and tries to regroup.'

Luke nodded and the two of them rode north.

The Outpost was not as far away as Luke had supposed. He didn't know how he missed it the last time he was on the ranch. It comprised a cluster of four small buildings, one of them rather larger than the others.

'We should go slowly. Likely he's got more men with him. You go round to the back of the large building. I'll stay here.'

When Sam judged Luke to be in position Sam hollered:

'Listen up, McTavish, we've got you surrounded. It's over. Come out with your hands up.'

His words were greeted by a rattle of gunfire. Luke counted at least six shots. Sam dived for cover. Luke didn't hear him return fire.

So, McTavish had brought more men with him. Luke grimaced. The building behind which he was standing was directly behind the one from where all the gunfire had come. He got down on his belly, crawled closer and peered in through a window.

Miranda was there, with three other women, one of them older than the rest; likely they were her sisters and her mother. What caused his heart to sink into his boots was the sight of Beaufort, Tobias, and their henchmen. They were using McTavish's family as human shields to prevent anyone from storming the Outpost.

'Hey you! Driscoll!'

Luke looked up on hearing a voice, to find that one of McTavish's men had sneaked up on him. The man made a move for his sidepiece but Luke was faster. Still kneeling on the ground he drew and fired, plunking the man right in the stomach. The cowboy gave a loud scream before falling over and turning the dirt red.

Luke dropped to all fours and moved as fast as possible away from the window. Too late. Someone had spotted him. Shouts went up from behind.

'Here's one, trying to get a sneak peek!' yelled one voice.

'Blast him!' shrieked another.

Shots rang out as Luke reached the safety of another building, which seemed to be a bunkhouse. He didn't make it unscathed: one bullet ricocheted and grazed his leg. The pain bit into him and he gritted his teeth. A quick check showed the bullet hadn't gone in. Unlike his brother's, his wound was clean. He was safe and alive – but for how long? Another fusillade of bullets put holes into his hiding-place and he hit the floor.

If Sam had gone down Luke knew it was only a matter of minutes before he himself was killed.

CHAPTER 20

Luke counted his heartbeats between shots: eighteen . . . nineteen . . . twenty, then he exhaled. There must be enough of McTavish's men to surround him; he wondered whether they were moving into position to do that, or did they think he was dead?

He couldn't hang about, waiting to find out.

Luke decided to spring up and rush outside, going down, if Fate so decreed, in a hail of glory. He checked his Colt and was about to charge through the front door when he heard the loud crack of a rifle and a stern voice demanding:

'Robert McTavish, come out now. This is your last warning.'

It was Sam; he was alive!

Luke gave a quick glance outside. His suspicions were confirmed: McTavish was moving the men who were now his bodyguards to surround him. Beaufort, Tobias, and the other two gunmen, Jeffro and Clay, were circling him, but Sam's ultimatum had now distracted them. Luke gripped his Colt and charged through the door, catching one of McTavish's men by surprise. The would-be ambusher jumped high as Luke fell on him, punching him square in the face, his fist bloody. Luke felt a tooth crack.

Belatedly, he saw that the man he hit was Tobias, the hired hunter. Tobias turned and spat blood.

'Damn!' he swore. 'That's the second time I've been hit in the mouth by a Driscoll. Your brother packed a bigger wallop, too bad he's dead.' The gunslinger gave a feral grin, mocking Luke. Enraged, Luke swung again but the smaller man anticipated the move and reared back. His own momentum caused Luke to lose his balance. Tobias drew a long slender blade.

So it was a knife fight he wanted. Luke would oblige him.

Luke pulled his own hunting knife, heavier than his opponent's and just as deadly. Tobias wielded his knife with deft skill, slashing and slicing to keep Luke at bay. Hunched in a crouch the wily outlaw prevented Luke from gaining an advantage. The two combatants slowly circled, each probing the other for weakness. Every few seconds Luke would lunge but his feints were easily blocked. When Tobias tried to get through Luke's defenses the big hunting knife proved an indomitable barrier.

All that was needed now was for Tobias to tire or let his guard down just a little, then Luke could get his knife in. A shout distracted Luke momentarily and Tobias lunged. Luke barely avoided the blade, which had aimed for his eye but nicked his shoulder instead.

'He's over here!' called Tobias. 'I've got him. He's mine.'

Luke looked up and saw Beaufort and McTavish appear at the opposite side of the bunkhouse.

'Don't toy with him – finish him off,' McTavish shouted, red-faced.

'Relax, McTavish, he's not going anywhere,' said Beaufort, a sly smile on his face. 'Tobias is an expert knife fighter. Never seen him get beat yet.'

'Did you take care of that marshal?' Tobias asked. Seeing his chance Luke made a lunge. He almost got his knife to his opponent's throat, only to have it knocked away at the last second.

'Never mind that, focus on Driscoll. I want him dead. The fool can't help but meddle.'

'I've got him!'

It seemed that Tobias was correct. After Luke's thrust Tobias had kicked out with his feet and slashed wildly. The twin attacks threw Luke off balance again and Tobias closed to press his advantage. Sweat poured from Luke's face, his breathing became labored. Tired, he was thinking: *if I beat Tobias I have to face Beaufort and the rest, possibly alone.* It would be an impossible task.

As Tobias's knife edged closer tiny nicks and cuts appeared on Luke's arms and legs. Luke rethought his tactics, searching in vain for an opening. Tobias sensed his opponent's desperation and closed in for the kill. In his mad rush to finish off the tired rancher Tobias left himself open. Luke saw a vulnerable spot and tried one last desperate gamble.

Flipping his knife so as to hold it point first, he threw it in one swift motion. The big hunting knife, not balanced for use as a throwing knife, nevertheless found its mark. Turning end over end, it landed in Tobias's throat.

Too late Tobias had tried to block the blade's thrust; Luke's throw was so strong that the knife had broken through the outlaw's desperate defenses. Tobias was on the ground, a pool of blood speading near his body.

The shock of Tobias's unexpected demise prevented either McTavish or Beaufort from reacting, though Luke didn't wait to find that out. He quick-drew and fired, hitting Beaufort in the arm. The gunman gave a shout and took flight, followed closely by McTavish. Another man stepped in front of Luke as he tried to pursue, blocking his path. Luke recognized him as McTavish's big foreman, Zack.

'The man who burned down my brother's house, eh?' said Luke, bracing himself for the big man's punch. It came, square on Luke's face, but only half-heartedly. Luke blinked the tears away and smiled. 'My turn, Zack.' He leveled the man with a punch to the gut. Then, bending over him, Luke took his knee to the foreman's face, leaving him semi-conscious on the ground.

But Zack's move had been partly successful, delaying Luke long enough for his boss to get away. Luke looked around, trying to see if there were any more of McTavish's men lying in wait. Seeing none, he set off again. Both McTavish and Beaufort were fleeing from the Outpost, the latter holding his left arm in pain. Luke thought of going after them; then he remembered Miranda, and went back to the building where he had seen her with the other women of her family.There he saw Sam outside standing over two dead bodies. The other hired gunmen, Luke surmised.

'I took care of two of them myself. How many are left?' he asked.

Sam shrugged. 'I couldn't find McTavish, but I don't see anyone else here. Frank came down to give a hand and said he'd nailed two of them.'

'I saw McTavish, and the last of the hired gunmen. They're headed north. Where is Miranda?'

'I'm here, Luke.' The door flew open and out came Miranda, tears in her eyes, followed by her mother and sisters. 'Oh Luke, it's been horrible. Daddy has been completely crazy. He kidnapped us and held us here.' She began to weep softly.

'Don't worry, Miranda, it's all over now. We still have to bring your father to justice, though. He did a bad thing.'

'Please don't hurt him. He's my father still, despite everything.'

'Don't worry, ma'am; we'll make sure he's treated fairly, as long as he surrenders quietly,' said Sam. 'Come on, Driscoll, we'll let Frank care for them. Show me where McTavish is.'

They found McTavish and Beaufort in a shallow gully four miles from the Outpost. Exhausted, they had run all the way. Luke and Sam had had the luxury of commandeering the horses that their quarry had left behind. The pair rode to the lip of the gully, where Sam shouted down:

'Game's up, McTavish. Surrender and come in peacefully. You'll get a fair trial.'

'Never!' came back the defiant reply.

This isn't going to end well, thought Luke as he followed Sam down the short slope into the gully. Beaufort quickdrew, hitting the marshal in the shoulder. Sam gave a shout and fell off his horse.

Luke charged ahead; the gunslinger aimed at him but, unable to get a shot off, he turned and started to run. Luke leapt from his horse on to the bounty hunter's back and dragged Beaufort to the ground, pummeling him all the way. Luke hit him hard in his left arm, right where he had shot him. Beaufort howled in pain and bucked trying to get Luke off him. The gunslinger was manic now, thrashing and lashing out, but Luke held on, driving the man further into the ground.

Then Luke felt a massive kick to his ribs. Grunting, he released his hold on Beaufort and rolled over to see McTavish standing above him, a gun in one hand. Luke grabbed a handful of dirt; he threw it, temporarily blinding McTavish, and used the distraction to get to his feet. The gunslinger had righted himself, and was going for his holstered gun.

'This is over, cowboy!'

'Danger finally found you, eh, gunslinger?' asked Luke, facing the battered and beaten man. Beaufort grinned at him and took aim. He was too slow. Luke quick-drew and gunned him. Three bullets hit the man's chest before he could get one shot off.

Luke had turned on McTavish before the gunslinger's body even hit the ground. The ranch owner started to back away, fear showing on his face.

'Just you now. No more hired hands or gunslingers. Give it up and you'll get a fair shake at trial.'

McTavish was holding his head in his hands, moaning.

'You idiot, you have no idea what you've done. You've ruined me.' He fired his derringer, but his hand shook, diverting his aim. The shot went wide. Luke ran forward, closing the distance between the two men. McTavish lost his nerve, screamed and tried to get away, but Luke was on to him, tackling him to the ground. He started punching the rancher over and over again.

'That's for my brother, and that's for Miranda, and this one is for me. Had enough yet?'

'Easy, cowboy. I think that about does it,' Sam said. He walked up and put his hand gently on Luke's shoulder. Shaking, Luke struggled to control his emotions.

'Yeah, I suppose.' He looked down at McTavish, who was lying on the ground, retching. 'I promised your daughter you'd live to see your trial. Now get up.' Luke grabbed the bloodied rancher by the coat.

McTavish, beaten, wearily got up with Luke's help.

'All right you win,' he panted. 'I surrender. Take me in.'

Luke glimpsed a movement out of the corner of his eye; it was too quick to follow, then he heard a shout.

'Luke, look out!' Before Luke could react McTavish had pulled another pistol from his waistcoat. Luke's eyes opened wide as he prepared for the fatal shot that would surely follow. The gun went off. Luke flinched and felt for the bullet hole. Nothing. Then he saw McTavish slowly slump to the ground, a hole in his forehead.

'Always check your prisoner for weapons, old lawman's trick,' said Sam quietly. He was holding a smoking pistol in his hand.

'Thanks, Marshal. I guess I owe you my life.'

'It's no problem, only doing my duty. I guess we'll have to explain this to his family.'

'I'll do it. I don't think there was any way that McTavish would have let himself be taken alive.'

Sam nodded, 'I agree. Come on then, we've still got a lot of work to do.'

Miranda, her sisters, and their mother cried rivers of tears when Luke broke the news that Robert McTavish was dead. Sam sent a couple of his men into town to arrest the sheriff for putting out fake Wanted dodgers, and rounded up another small posse to help with the prisoners and the dead. Luke accompanied the McTavish women to the main house. That evening they held a small funeral service for Robert, burying him in a small grave near his beloved ranch house. The next day the marshal's men prepared to leave for Austin; ten of McTavish's men had surrendered and confessed to conspiring to steal land and attempted assault on peace officers, and were leaving with them.

'Thanks for everything, Sam,' said Luke, shaking the marshal's hand.

'All in a day's work. Let me know what else we can do for you. In the meantime I hope everything works out for you.'

'Yes, I hope so too.' Sam saddled up and led the procession of arrested men, deputies and local townsfolk who had recently been temporarily deputized to help them. After he'd watched them leave Luke stepped back into the house. Inside he saw Miranda and her mother poring over papers in McTavish's former study.

'Look, Luke, this must be the reason that Papa was so adamant about getting your brother's land. He had gambling debts,' said Miranda.

'Debts a mile high,' added her mother. 'I cannot believe he kept this hidden from me, from all of us.'

Luke looked at the ledger and saw the staggering

amount of debt, owed to casinos in New Orleans, and riverboats on the Mississippi, all coming due soon.

'How will you pay this all back.'

'No choice for it, we'll have to sell the ranch. It's an easy decision now that Robert is gone. I'll move back East with the two younger girls.'

'Oh Mama,' wailed Miranda, 'what will become of me? I never much liked city living.'

Her mother gave Luke a knowing look and Miranda blushed.

'I'm sure this fine gentleman here will find a way to provide for you,' said Mrs McTavish. 'What may your plans be, Mr Driscoll?'

'Hum, now that I think on it, I don't rightly know. I guess I'll help Maryanne get the ranch back to what it was, then talk to Miss Miranda about what she wants to do. That is if she'll have me as her husband.'

Miranda gave a squeal of delight, quickly followed by her sisters' equally rapturous screams. Her mother only smiled pleasantly. 'So I take it that's a yes,' said Luke.

A big grin, as wide as the Montana sky, played over his face.